THE SISTERS GRIMM

5

THE S
GRI

10th Anniversary Edition

5

STERS
VIM

MAGIC AND OTHER
MISDEMEANORS

MICHAEL BUCKLEY

Pictures by PETER FERGUSON

AMULET BOOKS   NEW YORK

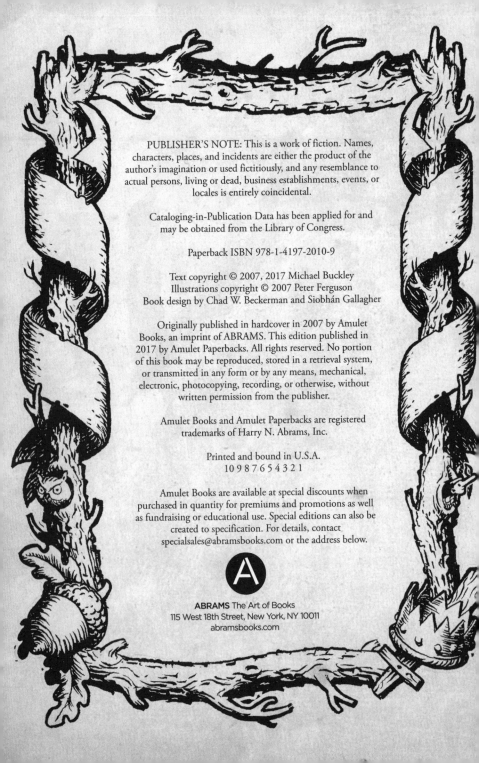

Cataloging-in-Publication Data has been applied for and may be obtained from the Library of Congress.

Paperback ISBN 978-1-4197-2010-9

Text copyright © 2007, 2017 Michael Buckley
Illustrations copyright © 2007 Peter Ferguson
Book design by Chad W. Beckerman and Siobhán Gallagher

Amulet Books and Amulet Paperbacks are registered trademarks of Harry N. Abrams, Inc.

Printed and bound in U.S.A.
10 9 8 7 6 5 4 3 2 1

Amulet Books are available at special discounts when purchased in quantity for premiums and promotions as well as fundraising or educational use. Special editions can also be created to specification. For details, contact specialsales@abramsbooks.com or the address below.

ABRAMS The Art of Books
115 West 18th Street, New York, NY 10011
abramsbooks.com

For Alison.

You put a spell on me.

Puck flapped his wings hard, but he couldn't resist the pull of the black, gaping hole above him. He looked like a worm struggling to avoid a hungry catfish's jaws.

"Hello! We've got a problem!" he cried as he flailed in midair.

Sabrina saw he was about to be swallowed and did the only thing she could think to do. She grabbed Puck's foot as he sailed past, attempting to stop his ascent. Unfortunately, she, too, was jerked off the ground. She cried out, but her grandmother, her uncle, and Mr. Canis were too far away to reach her. Only Sabrina's sister, Daphne, was nearby. The little girl latched onto Sabrina's pant leg only to be yanked off the ground as well. Now all three of them were caught in the hole's swirling gravitational pull.

Puck's face passed through the event horizon and his head completely disappeared. His upper torso and arms followed, then his waist, and finally his legs. All that was left of him in this world were his sneakers. Sabrina clung to them with all her strength.

"We're losing him!" Daphne cried desperately.

"Puck, you have to fight it!" Sabrina shouted.

But her own words sounded laughable in Sabrina's ears. How could he fight something with such power? What could any of them do to save themselves—and soon the rest of the world—from being sucked into nothingness?

Puck's shoes disappeared into the hole, though Sabrina could still

feel them in her hands. She knew if she let go he would be gone forever, so she hung on tight, even as she herself was swallowed. Both her
arms sank into the empty, dark pool. She took a deep breath and said
a final, silent prayer for her soul, hoping that God would find her on
the other side, wherever that might be.

And then the hole quadrupled in size.

1

Four Days Earlier

I'M SURE THIS COULD BE CONSIDERED CHILD ABUSE," Sabrina groaned. How many children had grandmothers who woke them up by banging a metal pot with a spoon? Granny Relda was like a member of the world's most annoying marching band.

"Sorry, *liebling*, but this is the only way to wake your sister," Granny replied in her light German accent. "Up and at 'em!"

Sabrina rolled over and eyed her seven-year-old sister, Daphne. The two of them had shared a bed for some time now, and Sabrina was well aware of how soundly her little sister slept. Daphne could doze undisturbed through a category-five hurricane, so Granny was forced to resort to unusual methods to wake her. It usually involved the most ear-shattering chaos she could create. To end the racket and save her own eardrums, Sabrina vigorously shook Daphne until her eyes opened.

"Whazzamattawitalllthebangin?" Daphne grumbled.

"It's time to start the day," Granny said, finally setting down her pot and spoon.

The old woman was fully dressed, wearing a bulky coat, mittens, a scarf, and boots. She might have looked as if she were going whale hunting if not for her bright pink hat with a sunflower appliqué in its center. "We've got to get in a little escape training before everyone arrives."

Both girls groaned.

"Granny, we hate escape training. We're no good at it," Daphne complained.

"Nonsense," the old woman said, pulling back the blankets and helping the girls out of bed. "You're both very good at it."

"Then how come we've never escaped?" Sabrina grumbled.

Granny did her best to hide her smile, then turned to exit the room. "Get dressed, girls. There is no time for dillydallying."

"What should we wear?" Sabrina called after her.

"Something warm. Something very, very warm."

The girls had come to understand their grandmother well in the time they had been living with her. If she said to dress lightly, that meant wear as little as possible. If she said to bring a towel, that meant bring a dozen. If she said to dress warmly, that meant two pairs of long johns, four pairs of socks, heavy blue jeans, boots, two sweaters, scarves, mittens, and a down coat. "Very, very warm" might well mean they should bring a portable space heater.

The girls helped each other into thick sweaters, heavy pants, and puffy coats. Sabrina added a wooden sword to her ensemble, shoving it into her belt. Puck had left it in the living room the night before and she had snatched it for her own.

"What's that for?" Daphne asked, eyeing the weapon.

"I'm tired of his surprises," Sabrina said. "This time I'm going to be ready."

Daphne nodded knowingly.

With mittens, scarves, and earmuffs in place, the girls stepped into the hall just as their uncle Jake opened the bathroom door. He smiled and said hello. He was a handsome blond man, lanky, with a crooked nose he'd earned in a fistfight. He was still in his pajamas and had a toothbrush hanging out of his mouth.

"Good luck," he said, giving them a thumbs-up.

"Easy for you to say," Sabrina mumbled. "You're not spending your morning running from a psychopath."

"You say that like it's not going to be any fun," Uncle Jake said with a wink, then he ducked back into the bathroom.

Granny was waiting for them in front of a door at the end of the hall. She sorted through a gigantic key ring that must have held a hundred keys—made of gold, silver, crystal, brass, even a skeleton key that looked like real bone. After finding the one she wanted, she clicked the door open and led the girls inside.

The spare room remained locked because it contained three very valuable things: an ornate, full-length mirror and Sabrina's sleeping parents, Henry and Veronica Grimm. They lay peaceful and still on a queen-size bed Uncle Jake had set up for them. The trio's arrival didn't disturb their sleep in the least. It was deep and, unfortunately, enchanted. Nothing the family had tried could wake Henry and Veronica up. Sabrina was desperate to break the spell that kept them unconscious, but Granny's training sessions kept getting in the way.

The old woman buttoned her coat and turned to the mirror. "Mirror, mirror, the morning is blessed. We're here to train. Are you dressed?"

The reflection in the mirror rippled the way the water does when a rock is thrown into it. Clouds and lighting appeared in the glass, as did an enormous face with an intimidating expression, which quickly brightened into a big smile.

"Bright-eyed and bushy-tailed," Mirror said. "Puck is ready for you. Sorry, girls, I tried to get some clues about what he has planned, but he was tight-lipped."

"Thanks for trying," Daphne said.

"The girls are not supposed to know what he's up to, Mirror. I'm trying to teach them how to prepare for the unpredictable."

"Well, you've chosen the right assistant in Puck," Mirror said.

"Shall we get started, girls?" Granny asked, nudging them toward the reflection.

Daphne reached out to touch the mirror, and her hand slid right through the surface. The image shuddered as Daphne stepped through the reflection and vanished.

"I hope there will be hot cocoa after this," Sabrina said to her grandmother with a grumble.

"I think I can arrange that," the old woman said. She took Sabrina's hand and together they stepped through the mirror, too.

The trio found themselves in a brilliantly lit space, a hallway that seemed as huge as Grand Central Station, with enormous marble columns holding up a barreled ceiling high above their heads. The hallway seemed to go on forever and was lined with hundreds of doors. Waiting for them was a short man in a black tuxedo. He had thinning hair and a soft, kind face. This was Mirror's true face, a far cry from the stormy brute that appeared on the other side of the glass.

"Good morning, Mirror," Sabrina said.

"Look at my little snow bunnies," Mirror said as he clapped his hands with glee. "Are you ready for your escape training?"

Daphne grumbled something under her breath.

"They're both a little tired," Granny explained.

"And hungry," Daphne said.

"The sooner we get started the sooner you can eat," Granny promised.

As Mirror led the group down the hall, Sabrina studied the space. Each doorway was a different shape and size, and many were made from unusual materials. Some were ordinary wood and steel, but others were made of bone, ice, rock, and even fire. A little brass plaque labeled each room: MAGIC CARPETS, UNICORNS, ENCHANGED ARMOR, GOLDEN FLEECES, LIONS, WITCHES, WARD-ROBES—the doors went on and on.

"Granny, how far does this hallway go?" Sabrina asked. "Does it just go on forever?"

"Oh, no," the old woman said. "There's an ending, I promise. But it would take you many days to get there on foot."

"Of course, the hall gets bigger if needed," Mirror said proudly.

Finally, the group stopped at a door with a plaque that read THE SNOW QUEEN'S KINGDOM. Granny handed Mirror her keys, and he went to work unlocking the door.

"Wait a minute. There's an entire kingdom behind this door?" Sabrina asked.

"Indeed," Granny said. "The Snow Queen's homeland is under lock and key in the Hall of Wonders."

"Why?" Daphne asked.

"At the time, it was decided that it was safer to capture her entire kingdom rather than try to hunt her down."

"Hunt her down? I saw the movie, Granny. She's just misunderstood, and there's a singing snowman!" Daphne said.

"That was the movie, *liebling*," Granny said. "The real story of the Snow Queen is a bit more . . . troubling. Hans Christian Andersen's accounts of her crimes—"

"Crimes?" Daphne cried.

"Oh, yes. She froze several people to death," Mirror explained.

"Now, Mirror, she has paid her debt to society," Granny interrupted. "She's settled down now. She lives on Beechwood Avenue near Old MacDonald's farm. I think she drives an ice-cream truck. But her kingdom is still too dangerous to release."

Mirror opened the door, and a bitter wind blasted the group. Sabrina swore she could feel icicles forming on her back teeth. She looked up at her grandmother. "Are you crazy?"

"This is going to be fun," the old woman said as she stepped inside.

"Good luck! I'll thaw you out when you get back," Mirror said as he nudged the girls through and closed the door.

Sabrina glanced around at the frozen wasteland. Everything was covered in ice. The ground was rock hard. Even the forest that stretched out before them was frozen stiff.

"My eyelashes are sticking together," Daphne said.

"Go on, girls," Granny said, pointing to a path that led up a hill bordering the dark wood. "You know how this works. Walk up the path. When you hear my whistle, you'll know you've gone far enough. Then turn around and try to make it back to me as quickly and cleverly as you can. Use your brains, and remember: The simplest way may not be the best way."

Sabrina knew arguing was pointless, so she took her sister by the hand and started down the path. They hadn't gone more than a few yards when they heard laughter echoing through the woods.

"He knows we're here," Sabrina said.

"This is all your fault," Daphne replied.

"My fault?" Sabrina asked. "How is this my fault?"

"You called him an ugly freak baby at dinner last night. Now he's out for revenge."

"It was a term of endearment."

After a while, the girls heard their grandmother's whistle.

"There it is," Sabrina said. They stopped and looked around, expecting Puck to attack at any second, but when he didn't appear after several moments, they turned to head back down the path. "Let's go."

A moment later, they heard more laughter and the sound of flapping wings. Suddenly, there was a loud explosion on the path next to them, resulting in a horrible smell and tons of green smoke.

"Your ugly freak baby is here," Daphne said.

Sabrina grimaced. Daphne was right about Puck. Sabrina teased the boy too much, and now he was going to make her regret it. Not that it was her fault. Puck's immaturity and disdain for personal hygiene made him an easy target—and besides, he gave as good as he got. The Trickster King, as he often called himself, was a four-thousand-year-old fairy and the master of obnoxious pranks, vulgar manners, and dirty tricks. He made himself the bane of Sabrina's existence. How was she supposed to know he couldn't take a little teasing?

There was another explosion, sending the girls darting behind an enormous tree. Sabrina peered around the trunk for Puck. He was nowhere to be seen, but she could hear his beating wings over the chill wind.

"He's booby-trapped the path," Daphne said, shivering. "We should go through the forest."

Sabrina studied a bank of fir trees several yards off the path. Daphne was right. They were thick and would make good cover, but something about them seemed too easy.

"He wants us to hide in the forest."

"Hiding is good," Daphne said. "I'm a big fan of hiding."

"I bet the first two explosions were the only ones on the path. He thinks we'll take to the woods. The rest of the path is probably clear."

"And if you're wrong?"

Sabrina furrowed her brow and thought, searching through her mental filing cabinet from her time in foster care. Granny might have been trying to teach them to think on their feet, but Sabrina and Daphne already had plenty of practice. Sabrina liked to think of herself as "queen of the sneaks" and had gotten the girls out of a lot of tough situations. Puck wasn't the only wily one in the Grimm household.

"I'm not," Sabrina said. "Puck wants us to run into those woods because he's set up something even worse in there. I'm not falling for it."

Daphne's face crinkled as if she'd bitten into a sour pickle. "So you want to stay out in the open? That's your plan?"

"And run really fast," Sabrina added.

Daphne peeked around the corner, then turned back to her sister. "I don't know about—"

But Sabrina didn't give her sister time to think about the plan. She grabbed Daphne by the hand and dragged her back to the path. Sabrina's hunch seemed to be correct. The rest of the path was not riddled with booby traps. Could they have actually out-tricked the Trickster King?

Soon, they came across a chunk of ice as big as a car. They stopped to catch their breaths and hid behind it with their backs pressed against its frozen surface. Sabrina took the opportunity to make sure the little wooden sword was still in her belt.

"Sabrina. You're a genius. I think we actually did it," Daphne said, peeking around the frozen boulder. "You're mucho smart-o."

"Mucho smart-o?"

"It's my new word," Daphne said. "It means you're very smart."

"In what language?"

"Daphne-ish," the little girl said matter-of-factly. Sabrina's sister was always coming up with odd little words or sayings. No one had any idea where they came from, but Daphne seemed to have a new one each week.

"You're really good at thinking on your feet," she added. "I wish I was better at it."

"Well, you're good at the magic stuff. I wish I could use a wand," Sabrina admitted. "I guess I'll do what I'm good at, and you'll do what you're good at."

"We make a pretty good team," Daphne said, hugging her sister.

"We do," Sabrina agreed, smiling.

"Isn't this just the sweetest moment?" a familiar voice said from above, with a mischievous snicker. "I'm going to get a cavity."

"Puck," Daphne groaned.

Sabrina craned her neck to get a good look at the boy. He was standing on top of the ice boulder wearing a grungy green hoodie and jeans covered in mud, food, and heaven only knew what else. His shaggy hair bounced in the wind, and he wore a devilish smirk on his face as if he knew something the girls didn't. He held a coconut-shaped device that looked a lot like a grenade. He had half a dozen more of them strapped to various parts of his body.

"What's that in your hand, Puck?" Sabrina asked suspiciously.

"Oh, this? It's my latest creation. I call it a glop grenade. Allow me to demonstrate," Puck said. "All you do is pull the pin, count to three, and throw. The unfortunate moron in its path is sprayed with all manner of disgusting rubbish. This one is filled with hairballs and chili. You'll have to take a lot of showers to wash it all off. You'll probably have to burn your clothes, too. So, where was I? Oh, yes . . ."

He pulled the pin.

Sabrina lifted her hands to show him they were clenched into fists. "You throw that thing at us, and it will be the biggest mistake of your miserable life, fairy boy."

"One," Puck continued, unimpressed.

"I mean it, you . . . you ugly little freak baby!" she shouted. She couldn't help herself.

"Two." Puck wound up, and with reflexes she hadn't even known she had, Sabrina snatched her wooden sword and brought it down on his hand. Puck cried out and dropped the grenade. It rolled to the base of a tree, where it blasted the bark with an icky brown-and-yellow slime. The frigid air quickly hardened the substance into an icy shell. Unfortunately, the air couldn't freeze the revolting smell.

"You're going to pay for that, snotface," Puck snarled, but Sabrina was already on her feet, pulling Daphne down the path.

"Look at the piggies run!" she heard him cry. "Silly piggies! You can't outrun me."

He was probably right, but Sabrina was going to try. She ran as fast as she could, stumbling as she lost her footing over and over again on the slippery terrain. Daphne was having just as much difficulty.

"One! Two! Three!" she heard Puck shout, and another foul-smelling grenade exploded just inches behind them.

"C'mon!" Daphne yelled, suddenly diverting the sisters into the forest.

"No! That's where he wants us to go!" Sabrina cried.

"We don't have any other choice," Daphne said as another grenade blasted all over the tree next to them.

They ran through an outcropping of tightly packed maples. Sabrina hoped the trees would provide the girls with cover for a moment so she could figure out what to do next. But her hopes were dashed as soon as she looked up. Hiding in the branches was an army of chimpanzees dressed in white-and-gray camouflage overalls. Each chimp wore a matching soldier's helmet and was holding one of Puck's glop grenades in its long, furry hand.

"OK. No sudden movements," Sabrina said, recalling her first encounter with Puck's primate privates. They were a nasty bunch and wouldn't hesitate to attack, but if the girls were very careful, they might be able to sneak away. "Just be quiet and take a slow step backward."

Daphne did as she was told while Sabrina kept an eye on the chimps. The beasts made no motion to attack. They just stared at the girls with a dull curiosity.

"They're going to let us go," Daphne said. "They're nice monkeys."

Sabrina cringed when she heard the first angry shriek.

"What did I say?" Daphne asked.

"They're not monkeys! And they're very sensitive about that!" Sabrina explained as the first of the grenades exploded at their feet, splattering the ground in what smelled like toilet water and mayonnaise. "Run!" she cried, reaching for her little sister.

But Daphne was already running back the way she'd come.

"Traitor!" Sabrina shouted, chasing after her. The chimps were in hot pursuit. They swung from limb to limb, screaming and spitting and tossing their disgusting weapons at the girls. Explosions went off all around, and the best the girls could do was cover their heads and keep running.

"Doing this without magic is mucho lame-o!" Daphne cried. "If I had the Shoes of Swiftness, we'd be out of here in a flash. I could even stop them with the Golden Cap. I'd like to see their hairy faces when a wave of flying monkeys descends."

"Just head back to the path," Sabrina said. As they approached the clearing, the chimps had fewer branches to swing from. It wasn't long before the dirty fur balls were tumbling out of the trees and falling into the huge snowdrifts below, forcing them to give up the chase. Sabrina glanced back and saw them shaking their fists at her and her sister.

Once the girls were on the path, they found themselves at the top of a steep embankment. At its bottom Sabrina spotted a thin black ribbon of smoke rising into the air. There was a fire burning at the bottom of the hill. When she squinted, Sabrina could see Granny Relda sitting next to it in a Victorian-style stuffed chair, her legs propped up on an ottoman. Sabrina couldn't help but grin, especially when the woman rose to her feet and waved. She seemed just as surprised as the girls that they had made it this far. A wave of pride rolled over Sabrina.

"We're going to make—"

Sabrina didn't get to finish her sentence. She lost her footing, flailing onto her back and sliding down the hill. In an attempt to steady herself, she'd grabbed Daphne's arm on her way down, but all it did was yank her little sister off her feet, too. Together, they hurtled down the embankment.

"No fair!" Puck cried as he swooped down over them, tossing one grenade after another. None hit their target—a lucky break for the girls, since there was nothing they could have done to avoid his attacks. They spun, flopped, skidded, and tumbled down the hill with no way to steer or stop. At the bottom, they slammed into their grandmother, knocking her off her feet.

"*Lieblings!* Are you OK?" Granny Relda asked.

"We're fine, Granny," Daphne replied. "Are you hurt?"

"I'm fine. Congratulations, girls. You passed the test!"

Suddenly, Puck appeared overhead with his last grenade in hand.

"No way! They cheated!" Puck whined.

"How did we cheat?" Daphne demanded.

"I don't know yet," Puck said.

"Puck, the girls beat you. There's no cause for sour grapes," the old woman said.

"I'll show you sour grapes," he said, tossing the last of his weapons. It hit the ground hard and rolled between Sabrina's legs.

"Puck, NO!" Granny shouted.

Sabrina cringed, expecting to be drenched in something disgusting. After a few moments, she opened her eyes, studied Puck's weapon, and smiled. The pin was still in place. She got to her feet, picked up the grenade, and pulled the pin.

"One," Sabrina said.

"Uh-oh," Puck said. "Put it down, piggy!"

"Two."

"I'm warning you," Puck growled. "I'll make you regret this!"

Sabrina didn't wait for three. She threw the grenade. It hit Puck in the chest, where it exploded in a purple burst that smelled like rotten eggs, pumpkins, and ranch dressing. The substance completely soaked him and then froze instantly in the frigid air, encasing him in an icy cocoon. His pink wings were still free, but the ice was too heavy. He plummeted to the ground with a thud.

Granny rested her hand on his frozen head. "We'll get you out lickety-split," she promised. Then, she opened a door, standing by itself in open space. "Go ahead, *lieblings*. You earned it."

Together, the girls stepped through the doorway into a welcome flood of warm air and bright light. Mirror and Uncle Jake were waiting on the other side.

"So, what's the verdict?" Uncle Jake asked.

Daphne beamed. "We passed!"

"Congrats, peanut," Uncle Jake cried, swooping up the little girl and planting a big smooch on her forehead. "I knew you could do it."

Mirror rushed to Sabrina and shook her hand vigorously. "Well done!"

"Thank you, Mirror," Sabrina said, her chest swelling up with pride. It was unusual for her family to praise her—not that she could blame them. In the past, she had been a cranky, argumentative jerk.

A third man interrupted the celebration, approaching from the mirror's portal at the end of the hall. He was enormous, standing nearly seven feet tall, with a shock of gray hair and bright gray eyes. His hands, one of which had dark black claws instead of fingers, were covered in fur, and a bushy tail hung out of the back of his trousers.

Mr. Canis hadn't always been a hairy giant. When the girls had first met him, he'd seemed like the frailest old man in the world, but he was changing, and not for the better. His new appearance reminded Sabrina that a monster called the Big Bad Wolf lived inside him and was slowly clawing its way out.

"Mr. Canis," Granny said. "The girls passed their escape test."

"I am pleased," Mr. Canis said, though his face didn't reflect his words. The old man did not smile often. "Relda, some of your guests have arrived."

"Oh dear me," Granny cried. "I'm not even finished cooking—oh, and Puck! Oh dear, Jacob, he could use a hand. He's just on the other side of the door."

Uncle Jake stepped through the doorway. A moment later he returned with Puck hoisted on his shoulder, still frozen solid.

"Where should I put him?" Jake asked, sniffing the boy. "Oh, mercy! He smells like a septic tank."

"Put him in the shower," Granny said. "The hot water will melt the ice, and he could use a bath anyway."

Puck mumbled angrily. Bathing was not one of his favorite pastimes.

"Stop your grumbling," Granny said to the boy. "When you're out of the shower, I'd like you to wear something clean. Perhaps that blue shirt with the cute little alligator on it that I bought for you."

Puck's unpleasant mumbling got louder.

"Puck, wear the shirt!" Granny Relda insisted. "We're having guests."

Daphne clapped her hands like a child at a birthday party. "The princesses are coming!"

The group walked back through the portal into the spare bedroom where Henry and Veronica rested. Uncle Jake carried Puck to the shower. Mr. Canis said he was going to get some rest, and Granny and Daphne rushed downstairs to greet the guests.

Sabrina, however, stayed behind, sitting down on the bed next to Henry and Veronica. They lay quietly, as if they were enjoying an afternoon nap. Sabrina ran her hand across her father's stubbly beard and kissed her mother on the forehead. A normal person might have been very disturbed by Sabrina's morning— flying boys, magical doorways, glop grenades, a wolfman, parents trapped under a spell—but for her, it was just another day in Ferryport Landing.

Sabrina's life hadn't always been so strange. Once, she was just a normal girl living in New York City with her family. There were times back then when she actually thought her life was boring. That all changed the night Henry and Veronica disappeared, with a bloodred handprint painted on the dashboard of their car as the only clue. The girls were placed in an orphanage and then the foster-care system, where they bounced from one crazy caretaker to the next—until Granny Relda showed up to take them in. Sabrina had been sure the old woman was just another whack-a-doodle. After all, according to Sabrina's dad, Granny Relda was supposed to be dead. Plus, the old woman was full of outlandish stories about their ancestors, Jacob and Wilhelm Grimm, and how their famous book of fairy tales was really a history of actual events. And she told them their new hometown of Ferryport Landing was also the home of all those fairy-tale characters, now known as Everafters.

Sabrina truly thought the old woman was off her rocker. Until Granny Relda was kidnapped by a giant.

The girls rescued her, and even more bizarre adventures followed. Soon, the girls were caught up in the fight to stop an evil group known as the Scarlet Hand from destroying the town.

Sabrina resisted her destiny for a long time. She wasn't interested in becoming a fairy-tale detective like her parents, her grandparents, and her ancestors before them. For Sabrina, the danger, chaos, and just plain craziness of the Grimm responsibility had taken some getting used to. Only recently, after a trip back to New York City, had she realized it was time for her to give the family business a chance.

Now, her days were packed with training: lessons on self-defense, crime-scene investigation, tracking, and the use of magical items. The latter was a class Daphne excelled in, but Sabrina didn't feel right around too much magic. She didn't like who she became when she used it—she was addicted, or "touched" as some of the Everafters said. Still, Granny felt it was important that Sabrina understood how magic worked and, especially, how to defend herself and her sister against it. The training was exhausting. But Sabrina was enjoying herself—especially when it came to things she excelled at, like clue finding and criminal psychology, both taught by former police deputies Boarman and Swineheart. All of it was fun . . . except for the glop grenades, of course.

As Sabrina sat on the bed, Mirror's face reappeared.

"How are the sleepyheads?" he asked.

"The same," Sabrina said with a sigh.

"Well, that's what the party is for. Maybe someone will have the key to waking them up."

Sabrina nodded hopefully. "Granny invited everyone who's ever been enchanted. Daphne is nearly jumping out of her pants. She's in a princess phase."

"All little girls have them," Mirror said with a smile.

"Not me," Sabrina said.

"Of course not. You're rough and tough," he teased.

She smiled. Unlike other magical items, Mirror was also a person—flesh and blood—even though he couldn't leave the confines of the Hall of Wonders. He was a good friend and confidant to Sabrina, and lately she turned to him more than anyone else. He always seemed to understand how she felt.

"By the way, you haven't told me what you want for your birthday yet. It's four days away," Mirror said. "It's not easy to shop when you're trapped inside a mirror, you know,"

"All I want is Mom and Dad," Sabrina said, looking at her parents. "Happy, healthy, and wide awake."

"It'll happen, sugarplum. Now, you better get downstairs. You've got to keep an eye on that uncle of yours. He's going through a princess phase of his own."

Sabrina laughed. "Was he always this girl-crazy?"

"He was worse," Mirror said with an eye roll as his head faded from the reflection. Sabrina leaned over, kissed her mom and dad on the cheek, and got up from the bed. "Just hang on a little longer," she told them. "We're going to find a way. I promise."

2

W HEN SABRINA CAME DOWNSTAIRS SHE found the house filled with guests: witches, princesses, a dwarf, and a few knights from King Arthur's round table. Everyone was munching on snacks and drinking punch while chatting with one another.

In one corner, Sabrina saw a familiar trio of women. They were known as the Three, a coven of witches who had worked for former Mayor Charming, cleaning up messes the Everafters didn't want the town's human population to see. One of the women was Glinda the Good Witch, whose life was chronicled in L. Frank Baum's *The Wonderful Wizard of Oz*. She wore an emerald-green pantsuit and held a wand with a crystal star on its end. The second woman seemed about a million years old. Her name was Frau Pfefferkuchenhaus, known from the Hansel and Gretel story. Rounding out the group was the beautiful Morgan le Fay, famous for her association with King Arthur. The Three were enjoying some soft cheeses while discussing the latest episode of their favorite televised dancing contest.

In another corner stood a diminutive man in a black suit whom Sabrina had encountered many times before. Mr. Seven, as he was called, was better known as one of the seven dwarfs. Like the Three, he used to work for Mayor Charming, but when the Queen of Hearts won the latest election he was out of a job. He smiled politely when he spotted Sabrina.

Sabrina smiled back, then turned to find Daphne sitting on the sofa wearing a shiny sequined tiara. Elvis, the Grimm's two-hundred-pound Great Dane, lay on the floor, resting his massive head in Daphne's lap. Snow White sat with them. Looking at the beautiful woman was like staring into the sunrise for too long. Snow was tall and radiant with eyes as blue as the summer sky. Ms. White wasn't just beautiful; she was also a kind and caring person, as well as an expert in judo, karate, kickboxing, and bow-staff fighting. Granny had hired her to come to the house three times a week to train the girls in self-defense. Ms. White had plenty of free time, since the Queen of Hearts had closed the school where Ms. White taught immediately after taking office. There was no news of when it would reopen, if ever.

In addition to being out of work, Ms. White was suffering from a broken heart. When she reunited with her former fiancé, William Charming, it seemed as if they were headed down the aisle at last. But the prince had disappeared after losing the election. Snow searched high and low for him, but it was as if he had vanished into thin air.

"Hello, Ms. White," Sabrina said.

"Huh? Oh, I'm sorry, Sabrina. Did you say something?" Ms. White asked as she stared blankly across the room. "I think I'm going to get us some wine. Who wants some wine?"

"Um, I'm seven," Daphne said.

"Of course you are," Snow White said, then rushed toward the kitchen.

"She's a little freaked out," Daphne explained.

"Why? What's wrong?" Sabrina asked.

Daphne pointed across the room toward a stunning woman with a dark complexion; eyes like hot chocolate; and a soft, shy smile. Her name was Briar Rose, though most knew her as Sleeping Beauty. Briar had been something of a fixture at the Grimm house lately. Uncle Jake had asked her for help finding a cure for Henry and Veronica, as Briar had plenty of experience with sleeping spells. It was a sincere request at the time, but since then Uncle Jake had developed a crazy crush on her that seemed to grow every day. When she walked into a room, he fumbled his words and tripped over things. Daphne, always the matchmaker, urged him to confess his feelings, but Briar was never without her overprotective fairy godmothers, Buzzflower and Mallobarb. The fairy duo did not like Jake, and they made it clear that they would turn him into a toad if they caught him so much as looking at Briar. Now, it seemed Jake wasn't the only person who was awkward around the princess.

"Briar used to be married to Billy Charming," Daphne whispered to her sister.

Uncle Jake entered the room, spotted Briar Rose, and nearly fell over the couch in his rush to talk to her. At once Buzzflower and Mallobarb blocked his path, as if they were linebackers protecting a star quarterback.

"Poor Uncle Jake," Sabrina said.

"He's got googly eyes for Briar," Daphne said as she gave Elvis's ears a good scratch. The dog's back leg tapped the floor happily. "You know what? I think we need to find Elvis a girlfriend, too."

Elvis got up with a snort and skulked out of the room.

"What did I say?" Daphne demanded.

"He must be a lifetime bachelor," Sabrina said.

Granny rushed to answer a knock at the door. Sabrina and Daphne watched as a young blond woman and an elderly man entered the house. Sabrina didn't recognize either of them.

"Cindy! Tom! What a pleasant surprise. Please come in," Granny said. "Let me take your jackets."

Cindy was another rare beauty. She had a button nose; high, freckled cheekbones; and a smile so bright it almost blocked out the rest of her face. Tom, on the other hand, must have been nearly eighty years old, with a gaunt face and shaking hands. He wore a tweed jacket and an old-fashioned felt hat. He leaned on a long brown cane and held a leather satchel close to his body.

"I hope we're not intruding," Cindy said.

"I heard about the get-together and insisted we come right over. I thought we might be able to help," Tom offered, setting his bag on the floor near the couch. "Even if not, we can at least do the dishes at the end of the night."

"Of course! The more the merrier," Granny said cheerfully. "Cindy, Tom, I think you know everyone here but my grand-daughters. Sabrina, Daphne, this is Mr. Baxter and his wife, Dr. Baxter."

"Are you Everafters?" Daphne asked hopefully, shaking the old man's hand.

Tom laughed. "Alas, I'm not, but my wife is."

Daphne raised her eyebrows and gazed at the woman.

"I'm Cinderella," Cindy admitted with an embarrassed smile.

Daphne let out a squeal so loud that everyone in the house fell silent and stared. Even Elvis bolted back into the room. The little girl bit down hard on the palm of her hand. It was an odd quirk she displayed when she was excited or happy or both.

"Yobubbaingalllah," Daphne said.

"Pardon?" Cindy asked.

"She's a little excited to meet you," Sabrina said.

Daphne took her hand out of her mouth. "I might barf!"

Cindy smiled. "It's very nice to meet you girls. Your father was—I mean, is—one of my favorite people."

"He has such a kind spirit," Tom added.

"We're big fans, too," Sabrina said, shaking the man's hand.

"Cindy hosts a radio program here in town," Granny explained.

"And we've got great news. We're about to go national," Tom said proudly. "We've been picked up by a radio syndication company. Soon *The Dr. Cindy Show* will be broadcast all over the country."

"Bravo!" Granny Relda said. "Your advice has helped a lot of people here in town. Now you can help even more."

"What kind of advice?" Sabrina asked.

"I help people settle family arguments," Cindy replied.

"She does more than that," Tom said. "Cindy has a natural ability to weed through disputes to find the root of the problem, and then she gives people tools and tips to help make things better. What she does is truly special."

"I had a challenging childhood," Cindy admitted. "I learned to deal with difficult people."

Sabrina watched the old man grab his wife's hand. He looked at her the way someone looks at a beautiful waterfall. Sabrina had seen that look on her parents' faces and in the photographs of her grandmother and grandfather. Cindy looked back at her husband with the same expression. *They've sure got googly eyes,* Sabrina thought.

Elvis let out a whine from behind the couch, where he was sniffing at the old man's satchel. Granny pulled the dog away by the collar. "Elvis, behave," she said. He snorted but did as he was told.

Just then, Puck made his entrance in typical fashion, stepping into the room and letting out a tremendous belch. "I'm here!" he announced, as if the crowd had been waiting for him all along.

"But I'm not a happy camper," he said to Sabrina. "I look like a fool." He was wearing the shirt Granny Relda had given him. It had a happy little alligator on it, but Puck had written I EAT PEOPLE in a word balloon above its head.

"It's a nice shirt," Sabrina said, trying to cheer the boy up.

Puck sneered. "'It's a nice shirt,'" he mocked. "I am the most diabolical villain in the history of the world. I cause chaos and disaster everywhere I go. I can't be seen in this silly shirt! For one thing, the alligator is smiling. If you want me to wear a shirt with a man-eating beast on it, the beast should be eating a man, not grinning like an idiot. This alligator looks as if it's ready for some birthday cake, not some poor man's leg! If Jonas the Betrayer ever saw me in this shirt, I would never live it down."

"Who is Jonas the Betrayer?" Daphne asked.

Sabrina shrugged.

"Well, I think everyone's here," Granny said to the group, stopping Puck before he could continue his tirade. "I know that you are all very busy, and it's not exactly a good time to be seen talking to a Grimm, so I'm grateful to each of you for taking the time to come and offer your help with our dilemma."

"Mayor Heart isn't going to tell us who we can and can't talk to," Morgan le Fay said.

The crowd murmured in agreement.

"Thank you," Granny said. "As you all know, my family has a reputation as problem solvers, but we've run into a problem that has us stumped. Today, I'm asking you to put your heads together and find a way to break the spell keeping my son and his wife asleep."

"I'm sure we can wake them up," Briar said, though the rest of the crowd didn't seem quite so certain.

Just then, there was another knock at the door.

"Oh, a late arrival. Sabrina, could you answer that for me?" Granny asked.

Sabrina hurried to the door, not wanting to miss a second of the meeting. She nearly fell over when she saw who was waiting on the other side. A decrepit old woman dressed in filthy rags peered at her from under bushy white eyebrows. She smelled of death and decay. Behind her, a run-down shack resting atop two enormous chicken legs paced around the front yard.

"Baba Yaga!" Sabrina gasped.

The old crone eyed Sabrina with an angry stare. "I was invited," she growled, pushing past her. A fold of Baba Yaga's black gown brushed against Sabrina's hand as she entered the house. It made the skin on her fingers feel as if she had just plunged them into a pot of boiling water.

Sabrina reluctantly followed the witch into the living room. Baba Yaga's arrival caused a few startled people to cry out, but Granny Relda welcomed her warmly and reminded everyone that Baba Yaga was wise and knew a number of magical secrets. After some grumbling, the guests agreed, and the party continued.

The guests went upstairs to peek at Sabrina's dozing parents. Some suggested this spell and that potion; others recommended a number of spirits or ancient druidic incantations. Granny Relda followed everyone around, jotting down each new idea in her spiral-bound notebook. A few guests even tried out a number of charms they had with them, but nothing worked. As the day turned into night, the suggestions petered out.

Before long, the meeting was over. The cookies were eaten and the punch bowl emptied. Everyone wished the Grimms luck before flying off into the night (some quite literally). Just before he left, Mr. Seven suggested that Charming's kiss might do the trick. Sabrina was willing to give it a try until Briar mentioned that the touch of Charming's lips might also make Veronica Grimm fall madly in love with him—as it had done with her. Blushing, Snow White and Cinderella both agreed.

"I'm sorry we couldn't be of more help," Tom apologized as he retrieved his bag from the living room.

"I'll think about it more," Cindy promised. "There has to be something that will work, right?"

Granny nodded, then showed the couple out. The Grimms were alone again, with no solution.

Discouraged, Sabrina crept up to bed. Uncle Jake followed with Daphne cradled in his arms. The little girl was sound asleep, and her tiara had slipped down around her neck.

"We're not giving up, 'Brina," Uncle Jake whispered as Sabrina pulled back the blankets.

"I know," Sabrina said, trying to fake a positive attitude.

Her uncle gave her a hug and left. Sabrina lay in the dark, waiting for her eyes to adjust, waiting for the little model airplanes that her father had built when he was growing up to come into view. She closed her eyes tight and fought back tears. She was so tired of waiting.

Later that night, Sabrina was suddenly roused from a deep sleep by loud banging on the door downstairs. She peeked over at her snoring sister and crawled out of bed.

"I'll get it," she grumbled.

With every step down the stairs, the knocking grew louder and more insistent. As Sabrina turned the doorknob, it occurred to her that maybe she shouldn't be opening the door in the middle of the night without an adult. But it was too late. She was already face-to-face with Baba Yaga.

"You are a thief!" the witch said, pointing her withered finger at Sabrina. An invisible force snatched the girl around the neck, lifting her off the ground and yanking her out of the house. "Give it back to me."

Sabrina couldn't breathe, let alone deny the witch's accusation. Helpless and lightheaded, she dangled above the grass, kicking her legs wildly.

"If you return what you took, I promise to kill you quickly," Baba Yaga added.

"Hag, Sabrina Grimm is under the protection of the Trickster King," a voice announced. Puck flew into the yard with his wooden sword in hand. He circled the witch while keeping an eye on her shack stomping around the front yard. "Leave her be, or you will face the wrath of the Blood King of Faerie; the Prince of the Wrong Side of the Tracks; the beacon of hope for all good-for-nothings, slackers, and delinquents; the spiritual leader of—"

Before Puck could finish his boasting, Baba Yaga raised her free hand. A blast of energy shot out of her palm and slammed into the fairy boy's chest. The impact was so powerful, he sailed across the yard and far into the field on the other side of the street.

The noise must have woken the rest of the family. Granny, Daphne, Uncle Jake, and Elvis charged outside.

"Put her down, Old Mother," Granny Relda demanded, though she was rather unintimidating in curlers and fuzzy slippers.

"Your nestling has stolen from me, Relda," Baba Yaga snapped.

"Put her down, witch," Uncle Jake said. "You're not the only one who can wield magic around here."

Baba Yaga sneered. "Your threats mean nothing to me. They're like a mosquito buzzing around. Hold still, and I'll swat you."

Suddenly, something big, brown, and furry raced out of the house, slamming into Baba Yaga and knocking her to the ground. The assault broke the witch's concentration, and the suffocating grip on Sabrina's throat vanished. She fell to the porch, clutching her throat, forcing air into her empty lungs. Tears filled her eyes, making the scene a blur, but she knew what had attacked the witch. Mr. Canis was out of his room, and he was angry.

"Why don't you swat me instead?" Canis said as he hovered over the hag. Baba Yaga shrieked in rage. She raised her right hand, and a ball of crackling energy materialized in her palm. Mr. Canis flew backward, slammed roughly against the house, and let out a pained groan. The impact was so violent, Sabrina was worried he wouldn't be able to shake it off. But with animal speed and reflexes, he leaped forward, snatched the witch off the ground in one of his huge hands, and tossed her at her own house. The crash was deafening. She smashed through the front wall of her shack, leaving a gaping hole between the two filthy windows. The shutters fluttered like eyelids.

Uncle Jake helped Sabrina to her feet. "What did you do that's got her so mad?" he asked.

"She thinks I stole something from her," Sabrina choked.

Baba Yaga appeared in one of her windows. "She has been touched!" she screamed, pointing directly at Sabrina.

"You're mucho crazy-o!" Daphne cried as she struggled to hold Elvis back from attacking the witch. "Worse, you're mean. My sister didn't steal anything from you. Leave her alone, or things are going to get ugly." The little girl assumed her attack position and made her warrior face—a slightly comical expression she believed people found intimidating. But Granny Relda nudged both Daphne and Elvis back inside.

"Give me what is mine, or I'll destroy this house and everyone in it," Baba Yaga demanded.

"We have no idea what you are talking about," Granny insisted.

"Merlin's wand!" the witch screamed. "Your nestling has stolen it."

"I didn't take anything from her!" Sabrina cried. "I wouldn't go back to her stinking house for a million bucks!"

"Liar! Thief!" Baba Yaga shrieked.

"I believe Sabrina," Granny said firmly. "Someone else must have taken it. If you want our help getting your wand back, all you have to do is ask, but you're not to come here and threaten my family. I don't care who you are."

Baba Yaga disappeared from her window. A moment later, she scurried into the Grimms' yard, pointing her gnarled, wart-covered finger at Sabrina. "She—"

"I have never lied to you, Old Mother," Granny interrupted.

Baba Yaga stopped in her tracks. She narrowed her eyes at Granny Relda, then Sabrina. "You will find the wand?"

Granny nodded. "We'll come out to see you in the morning, and we'll get to the bottom of this."

"Fine!"

"Fine."

The witch hobbled back into her house. A moment later it rose up on its chicken legs, turned, and lumbered away. It disappeared into the woods, leaving a trail of black chimney smoke in its wake.

Moments later, Puck swooped back into the yard and landed in front of Sabrina with his sword clenched tightly in his hand. "Where did she go?"

"She's gone," Sabrina said.

"Coward! Of course she ran off," Puck crowed. "She attacked

me when I wasn't ready and then ran back to her woods! Miserable sissy!"

"Well, you can settle your dispute with her tomorrow. We're going for a visit," Granny said.

Sabrina turned to her grandmother. "If you think I'm going to that woman's house again, you're as crazy as she is."

"This is crazy!" Sabrina shouted as she squished through the mud with her grandmother, Daphne, and Puck. An early morning rain had soaked the woods, turning the forest floor into a chilly swamp. Puck followed Sabrina, muttering to himself about what he planned to do to Baba Yaga when he confronted her, while occasionally remembering to insult Sabrina.

"I hear she eats people, Grimm," he said. "I bet she turns you all into jerky!"

"I don't want to be jerky," Daphne cried.

"No one is going to get turned into jerky," Granny said. "This is going to be nice and pleasant."

"That's what people always say before they become jerky," Puck said. "Don't worry, folks. I've got a score to settle with the witch. She'll regret the day she laid a hand on the Trickster King."

Puck's boasting made Sabrina nervous. Baba Yaga had a two-thousand-year-old reputation for black magic and even blacker moods. The family journals were filled with tales of her murders and cannibalism. The last time Sabrina had visited her creepy house, Baba Yaga turned her into a frog and tried to eat her. The last thing they needed was for Puck to pick a fight with the crone.

They walked until they came to a part of the forest where the thin, dead trees grew had grown close together, their limbs intertwined. Though there were no leaves to block the sunshine, the space was dark and gray. Not a blade of grass sprang from the ground. Sabrina realized the natural sounds of the forest were also gone: the scurrying of animals, the wind in the branches, the crackling of earth beneath their feet—all silenced.

The family continued on until they found themselves on a path made of what looked like bleached stones. Sabrina knew where it led—straight to the man-eating witch. She also knew that the stones of the path were not what they seemed. It wasn't long before Puck noticed as well.

"These are human skulls!" he cried, digging one out of the ground and holding it up to the group.

"Don't be frightened, Puck," Granny said.

"Frightened? This is the coolest thing I've ever seen! Can we make a path like this at our house?" the boy asked. He moved the skull's jaw up and down like a puppet and shoved it in Daphne's face. "Hey, little girl, how about a smooch?"

Daphne shrieked and hid behind her sister. Granny Relda scolded Puck, demanding he return the skull to the path.

"What happened to your revenge, Trickster King?" Sabrina asked. "All of a sudden Baba Yaga is cool?"

"Just because I'm going to unleash hellfire on her doesn't mean I can't appreciate her style," Puck said.

"Granny, what happened to the bodyguards?" Daphne asked as she peered ahead. The notorious Bright Sun, Black Midnight, and Red Dawn—each a bizarre hybrid of an animal and a man—usually guarded the old witch, but they were nowhere in sight.

"Don't worry about them," Puck said. "They won't be showing their ugly faces around here. They know better than to cross paths with me." His voice cracked at the end of the sentence. Puck looked around as if someone else had made the noise. He repeated the word "me" with the same result.

"Sounds like you might be coming down with a cold," Granny said.

"Everafters do not get colds!" Puck argued.

"Nonetheless, I'll make you some chicken soup later."

The group continued down the path and soon Baba Yaga's hut came into view. A fence made from ancient human leg and arm bones surrounded it. Granny Relda pushed open the gate and led the family into the yard. Sabrina eyed her grandmother with both awe and envy. The old woman was fearless. She strolled to the front door as if she were visiting an old friend. Sabrina wondered if she herself would ever be that courageous.

Granny knocked, and a moment later the door flew open.

"You're interrupting my soaps," Baba Yaga seethed. She was eating a bowl of cereal.

"I'm sorry," Granny Relda replied. "We thought you'd want us to get started as soon as possible."

The witch frowned but waved everyone into the house. The inside was as disturbing as the outside. In one corner, dusty burlap bags leaked green ooze onto the floor. Along the wall were stacks of crates, one of which seemed to have something inside struggling to break free. The brick fireplace was lit, and the flames formed the desperate faces of people begging for help. Sabrina shuddered to imagine herself trapped, suffering for eternity in Baba Yaga's home. Still, the most unsettling thing wasn't the filth and despair, it was the odd sensation churning in Sabrina's gut. At first she thought it was just nerves, but she soon realized it felt more like hunger—a nervous, unnatural craving. Every drop of blood and strand of hair in her being was wide awake and starving. She glanced around at the wands, spell books, and magical rings the witch had left lying about. Baba Yaga didn't deserve those things. Look how she misused and mistreated them!

"Are you going to be OK?" Daphne asked, squeezing Sabrina's arm.

Sabrina took a deep breath and nodded. "Let's get out of here as soon as we can."

"Where are your guardians, Old Mother?" Granny Relda asked the witch.

"They failed me," the witch snapped.

"That's not what I asked."

"Don't question me!" the witch screamed, enraged. "I created them for a purpose. They were to guard my possessions and prevent any invasion into my home. They failed. You needn't know more."

Sabrina easily read between the lines. Baba Yaga's guardians were dead. Their bones were probably part of the fence outside.

Puck, on the other hand, was completely oblivious to the conversation. He was busy snooping, opening cabinets and peeking into drawers as if he owned the place. "This book looks like it's made out of human skin!" he exclaimed when he picked up a discarded tome off the floor. The cover looked like leather, but had hair growing out of it.

"It is," Baba Yaga confirmed.

Puck beamed. "This place is like my Disneyland."

"Uh, hello?" Sabrina said. "What happened to the hellfire?"

Puck scowled and put the book back on the floor.

"Old Mother, tell us everything you know about your missing wand," Granny said as she took out her notebook and pen.

"It was here one moment and gone the next," the witch said, flashing Sabrina an accusing look.

"Can you show us where you kept it?" Granny asked.

The crone hobbled into the next room, where the floor was covered in dust and what looked like human teeth. An overstuffed recliner faced a television that was set up against the wall. The jawbone of some huge animal rested atop the TV with an old wire hanger wrapped in tinfoil sticking out of it, making a disturbing antenna. The TV was tuned to a soap opera called *Days of Our Lives.*

"I kept the wand in here," the witch said as she gestured around the room.

"OK, girls. Here's where we get to put your training into action," Granny Relda said. "Have a look around, and remember, keep an eye out for anything that's out of place."

In the last two months Granny Relda had been teaching Sabrina and Daphne to see—or rather, to observe—things. She believed good detectives used all of their senses to get the most accurate picture of a crime scene. Her method included sniffing for odd scents, listening for unusual sounds, and peeking into dark corners. Sabrina had her own method, though. She believed the best way to find a criminal was to think like one. All she had to do was think about what she might have done if she were trying to get away with something. When she combined her approach with her grandmother's, she discovered that she could spot things that others missed.

She scanned the room, wondering what her grandmother might mean by "out of place" in this room where everything was bizarre. Ancient wallpaper was peeling from the walls. Something reddish Sabrina hoped wasn't blood stained the floor. In the far corner, a table held little glass jars filled with greenish liquid. All manner of disgusting objects floated inside them.

"Sabrina?" Daphne said. "What do you see?"

Sabrina peered at the table but saw nothing out of the ordinary, if you considered a pile of dead chameleons ordinary. Still, Granny had taught her to be thorough, so she peeked under the table. There, she spotted a small hole in the baseboard. Daphne joined her and pointed out little greasy paw tracks and some wood shavings around the hole. The witch had mice chewing through her floors.

"When did you notice the wand missing?" Granny asked.

"Late last night," the witch said.

"Was anything else taken?"

"No," Baba Yaga snapped. "Do you know who did it yet?"

"We just got here," Granny said.

The witch scowled. "Tomorrow I will take matters into my own hands, Relda Grimm."

"Old Mother, please," Granny begged. "You have to give us some time."

"You heard me. Tomorrow!"

3

WHEN THE FAMILY RETURNED HOME, Granny sent the children to wash up while she prepared one of her signature dishes—corn flakes in avocado sauce. The old woman was under the impression that the recipes she collected on her adventures around the world delighted her whole family, but she was very, very wrong. Sabrina couldn't stand her grandmother's weird cooking. Day after day she suffered through tulip root soup, Chinese beetle bread, crocodile steaks, creamed bacon with butterscotch nuggets, horseradish-flavored oatmeal, Limburger pancakes, and more.

Sabrina might have been able to convince Granny Relda to tone down the menu if she weren't surrounded with people who would eat anything. Daphne scarfed down whatever was put in front of her, even dishes that Elvis refused. And Puck rarely looked at the food before shoving it into his mouth. That afternoon, the response was no different. Granny had to keep rushing back to the kitchen to refill Puck's plate. He even tried to steal a couple of rolls from Daphne, but the little girl used her fork to defend them.

"Puck! What is wrong with you?" Granny asked, exasperated.

"I'm starving!" the boy fairy cried as he shoved a celery stalk into his mouth. "I could eat a horse, and that's not a joke. I would know. I've eaten a horse!"

Daphne whimpered. She had a fondness for ponies.

"Arthenus the World-Smasher bet me I couldn't do it," Puck said between bites. "That rat still owes me a million dollars. He tried to back out when I wouldn't eat the saddle. The saddle is not technically part of the horse, is it?"

Everyone stared at the boy.

"Well, it's not, right?"

Mr. Canis entered the room and took a seat. He had grown several inches and packed on tens of pounds of muscle. Squeezing into his chair was getting harder and harder for him. Soon, Sabrina suspected, he wouldn't be able to join them for dinner at all.

"Mr. Canis, our friend Puck has some odd symptoms. Earlier his voice was cracking, and now he can't seem to get enough to eat," Granny said with a smile.

Mr. Canis examined Puck closely then sniffed in his direction. "Interesting."

Puck sat up and turned his head from the old woman to the old man. "What? What's wrong?"

Granny Relda smiled knowingly, then shrugged.

Puck scowled, then stuck out his tongue at Sabrina, exposing a mouthful of half-chewed food. He laughed when she gagged.

There was a knock at the door, and since Sabrina no longer had an appetite, she stood, handing her plate to Puck. "I'll get it."

At the door, she found Morgan le Fay, looking distraught.

"I need your help," she said. "I've been robbed."

Sabrina sighed. "I think I'm beginning to see a pattern."

Everafters unnerved Sabrina. She didn't like animals that could talk or inanimate objects that could scurry around. Trolls gave her the willies, and the memory of her encounter with Rumpelstiltskin still haunted her. But witches were the spookiest of them all. Most were covered in warts and oddly-placed puffs of hair. They smelled funny and laughed at things that were disturbing, not funny. Even the seemingly normal Glinda had a bizarre way of talking—a singsong that grated on Sabrina's nerves. All in all, she could have done without witches.

Morgan, on the other hand, was a beautiful, curvy woman with jet black hair and big bright eyes. She reminded Sabrina of the kind of women she sometimes saw walking around the East Village, wearing vintage house dresses, pumps, and bright red lipstick. She was undeniably cool; she was also funny, smart, and a little sarcastic, which, as a New Yorker, Sabrina held in the highest regard. Plus, she had a seductive charm that drove men of all ages crazy. Even Mr. Canis fumbled a little in her presence. Uncle Jake nearly knocked over the dining room table when Granny asked him to drive the family to Morgan's house to investigate the robbery.

The enchantress lived in a house not far from the Metro-North train station. The neighborhood was nothing fancy. The sidewalks were crumbling and the yards were filled with overgrown weeds and crabgrass. However, Morgan's house was immaculate. The lawn was perfect. Not even a stray leaf spoiled its landscaping. The porch was freshly painted and the walkway was lined with blooming flowers.

The family followed Morgan as she sashayed to her front door. Waiting on her porch were half a dozen men who quickly removed their hats, straightened their hair, and sucked in their potbellies. They begged for her attention.

"Morgan," one of the men said. "I fixed that leaky sink."

"Oh, Steven, you're a doll," Morgan said, kissing the man on the cheek. "I only called about it yesterday."

"Morgan, I've gone to the hardware store and picked up the paint for the living room," another man said proudly, as if he had just won a gold medal in the Olympics.

"Morgan, I'll be here bright and early tomorrow to change your oil," another man announced.

"Morgan, I put in a new hot water tank for you."

"Morgan, I fixed that crooked mirror in your bathroom."

"Morgan, I spackled that hole in the kitchen ceiling."

"Oh, boys, you really must let me pay you something for all the hard work you're doing," she purred.

"Absolutely not!" the men cried, then turned and shot one another angry, jealous looks.

"Boys, I'm so happy you came by, but I have some guests right now," the beautiful witch said. The men looked brokenhearted. They threw out a few halfhearted "OKs" and "of courses" and promised to return at a time that was more convenient for Morgan.

The witch unlocked her home and led the Grimms inside, where Sabrina was met with a terrific racket of rockets, machine guns, and helicopters. She could actually feel the floor rumbling beneath her shoes. She would've thought she'd just stepped onto a battlefield had she not noticed the very pale and pudgy man playing a violent video game. He looked to be in his late twenties, though his three-day beard, paunchy belly, and tired eyes made him seem much older. He wore a ratty T-shirt emblazoned the words ONE RING TO RULE THEM ALL. Pizza boxes and hamburger wrappers littered the floor. If he noticed the family's arrival, he made no sign of it.

"Mordred, honey," Morgan said, "we have company."

"Yeah, I see them," he said without turning his head.

"Well, turn off your game and say hello!"

MAGIC AND OTHER MISDEMEANORS

"Mom! I'm about to beat level fifteen! Do you have any idea how many experience points I will get?"

"Mordred, pause your game," she said.

"I can't. I have to finish this level," he whined.

"Mordred! Fine, if you don't want to act like an adult, then go to your room and clean it up. I have to vacuum in there, and you've got your dolls all over the place."

Mordred looked over at his mother in a murderous rage. His pupils vanished and his eyes turned pure white with energy.

"THEY'RE NOT DOLLS! THEY'RE ACTION FIGURES!"

Morgan leaned down and turned the television off. Mordred roared, leaped up from the couch, and slammed his controller on the coffee table.

"That's enough screen time for one day," Morgan said.

"The exterminator is in the bathroom," he snapped before marching out of the room and slamming the door behind him.

"I'm sorry about that," Morgan said. "Mordred is a bit aimless. He's had a difficult time holding a job lately, so he's been hanging around here. He's worked at Wendy's, Taco Bell, and Burger King, but it always ends the same way—he challenges his manager to combat, takes over the restaurant, and enslaves his coworkers. Then it's back to video games."

"We'd like to get right down to business, if possible," Granny said without batting an eye. "You told us you have been robbed. What was taken?"

"The Wonder Clock," Morgan le Fay replied as she walked around the room picking up empty french-fry boxes.

"No way!" Uncle Jake exclaimed.

"Uh, what's the Wonder Clock?" Sabrina asked. Her father had kept her and Daphne away from fairy tales when they were little, trying to protect them. It put the Grimm sisters at a disadvantage in Ferryport Landing.

"Howard Pyle wrote about it, *liebling*. According to his story, the Wonder Clock was kept in Father Time's attic," Granny explained, then turned her attention back to Morgan. "I was under the impression the Wonder Clock was lost during the Everafter pilgrimage to America."

"So was I!" Uncle Jake said.

"No," Morgan said as her cheeks turned pink. "I've had it all along."

"What in heavens for?" Granny asked. "Pyle's story says it's only function is to tell stories when the clock struck the hour. I understand the impulse to hide some enchanted items, but the Wonder Clock is barely more than a children's toy."

Morgan le Fay shuffled her feet. "Well . . . it does something else."

Uncle Jake grinned eagerly. "What?"

"It's kind of a time machine."

Sabrina laughed.

"No, really," Morgan said. "It lets a person go up to twelve hours into the past. All you have to do is wind the hands in the opposite direction."

"What good is that?" Daphne wondered.

"It comes in very handy when you accidentally say yes to two dates on the same night," the beautiful witch said.

"Morgan, how long has the clock been missing?" Granny asked.

"I'm not sure," the witch replied. "I came home from your party and went straight to bed. It was on the kitchen table when I turned off the lights. This morning it was gone."

"And you didn't hear anything?" Granny asked.

"Nothing at all. The front door was wide open when I woke up, but I know I locked it."

"What about Mordred?" Uncle Jake asked. "Could he have taken it?"

"No," Morgan said. "He says he has no idea what happened to the clock, and I believe him."

Just then, a fat orange creature no more than a foot tall stepped out of the bathroom. It was wearing green camouflage pants, a green shirt, an army helmet, dog tags, and heavy boots. At first glance, it looked like a dressed-up pet, but it was walking erect on its hind legs.

When the creature saw the family, panic swept its face. It shouted "Incoming!" and dove behind the couch.

"Boots, it's OK," Morgan said. "It's Relda Grimm and her family."

The animal peeked its head from around the couch, allowing Sabrina to give it a closer look. It was a cat. He looked nervous, and his whiskers were frantically twitching. "You scared the bejesus out of me," Boots said in a thick New Jersey accent. "I coulda' had a nervous breakdown. You gotta warn a guy. I'm a veteran. I've seen terrible things. Makes a guy jumpy."

"We're sorry, Boots. So, did you find anything?" Morgan asked. "Boots is an exterminator," she explained to the Grimms. "I'm embarrassed to say it, but I found evidence of mice this morning."

"Well, Ms. le Fay, I've got good news and bad news," Boots said. "I'll start with the bad news. You do indeed have mice."

"Ugh," Morgan groaned. "I knew it! One of them chewed through my purse." She reached into the bag and poked a finger into a small hole near the bottom. "What's the good news?"

"There is no good news. I just thought it might help to have some hope. My advice is to pack your things, burn this place to the ground, and start somewhere new."

"You want her to abandon her home because she has a mouse?" Sabrina said incredulously.

"It's the only chance you have. There is nothing you can do to stop vermin. They just keep coming and coming and coming, haunting your dreams, eating your cereal! Oh, the horror . . ." The cat gazed vacantly into the distance as if trapped inside a troubling memory.

"What's *vermin* mean?" Daphne whispered.

"Vermin are pests like rats, mice, or cockroaches," Sabrina explained.

Daphne's face contorted with disgust. "Gross!"

"I'm going to have to check the basement to make sure you don't have a nest," Boots said, though Sabrina could see he was visibly trembling. "I just need a minute to prepare myself. I didn't expect to have to go into the heart of darkness this morning."

Sabrina tugged on her grandmother's sleeve. "We saw a mouse hole at Baba Yaga's house," she reminded her.

Granny winked at Sabrina and then turned to Boots. "A mouse, you say? Mind if we take a look in the basement as well?"

"I have to tell you, Relda, this could get dangerous. We might not all make it back alive," Boots warned.

"From looking for mice in the basement?" Sabrina asked.

"They're vile, unpredictable creatures. They're all teeth, fur, and claws."

"We'll try to be careful," Granny Relda said.

"Don't say I didn't warn you," Boots said.

"What about my missing clock?" Morgan asked.

"It's possible this is all connected," Granny replied.

"If you find anything, please let me know," Morgan said to Uncle Jake, resting her hand on his arm. "Oh, strong."

"Yeah, I lift weights from time to time," he bragged.

Granny grabbed her son by the other arm and pulled him along. "You can be so embarrassing sometimes, Jacob."

Boots led the family down to the basement. When he unlocked the door, he raised a finger to his mouth. "Shhh! Be very quiet. They've got great hearing."

The basement was damp and cluttered. There were stacks of moldy cardboard boxes, a collection of poorly laced tennis rackets, an artificial Christmas tree still covered in tinsel, and an old coffee table with a wobbly leg. Boots weaved his way through the room, staring up at the cobweb-strewn rafters. He shined his flashlight along the walls and ceiling.

"What are you looking for?" Daphne whispered, peering into the shadows.

"Their headquarters," Boots purred. "Or a hole in the floor. They could be chewing their way through the wood. They're incredibly resourceful. They can squeeze through a hole a quarter of their size. They can chew through concrete and jump up to twelve inches in the air. Plus, they're ravenous. They've got to eat fifteen to twenty times a day. When you combine that with how many babies they make in a year—upwards of a hundred—you can see we are under assault. They're coming for us, kid. They're going to take over the world. It's not a matter of if . . . it's a matter of when."

Just then, Daphne brushed against a cardboard box, knocking it to the ground. There was a heavy thump and clang. Boots leaped behind a chair

"We're under attack!" he shouted.

Granny helped him up and assured him the invasion had not yet begun. When he calmed himself, he went back to his search.

"There's no holes down here, which is odd. They usually migrate to the dark parts of a house. It's possible Morgan carried it in from outside, maybe in her bag, or on her coat. A mouse can leap onto a coat and cling to it for days. They're sneaky. In fact, their name comes from a Sanskrit word for thief."

"Could it be something other than a mouse?" Uncle Jake asked.

"Like what?"

"Oh, I don't know—a little person, perhaps a Lilliputian?"

"Sorry, Jake, that's not my specialty, but anything's possible."

"Boots, have you gotten calls from any other residences about mouse problems today?"

"I haven't been at the office today. Maybe."

Granny reached into her handbag and found a pen and a small scrap of paper. She scribbled her phone number onto it and handed the paper to the cat. "Would you call us if there are any other invasions like this one?"

Boots nodded. "You on some big case, Relda?"

Granny smiled. "We are Grimms. This is what we do."

"I can't believe the effect that woman has on men," Uncle Jake said as they drove back through town. "Did you see all those guys waiting for her? They were falling all over themselves trying to get her attention."

"But not you, right?" Daphne said.

"Oh, please, I half expected you to offer to scrub her floors," Granny grumbled.

Uncle Jake laughed. "Don't worry, Mom. I'm not going to bring a witch into the family. I've got my eye on a princess."

"You should have your eyes on finding clues," Granny scolded. She turned in her seat to face the girls. "Well?"

Sabrina and Daphne gaped at her.

"What are you asking us for?" Sabrina sputtered.

"Because this is your case. You two are detectives. What have you detected so far?" the old woman asked.

Daphne shrugged, causing Sabrina to grimace. She was hoping her little sister had noticed something she hadn't.

"C'mon, girls," Granny prodded. "What do these two robberies have in common?"

"Stolen magical items," Daphne said.

"Correct!"

"Um, both were robbed by someone that the victims never saw?" Sabrina added.

"Excellent!"

"Both of the people who were robbed were witches," Daphne added.

"And both have a mouse problem," Sabrina said.

"So you have been paying attention," Granny said with a grin.

"You think mice broke into their homes and stole their stuff?" Sabrina asked with a snort. "You sound as crazy as that cat!"

"Um, hello? We're in Ferryport Landing," Uncle Jake said. "It's more than possible."

"The Three Blind Mice live on Main Street, and the Mouse King and his people live over by the river," Granny said. "In fact, there are quite a number of mice living in this town, but I have what we detectives call 'a hunch.'"

"You know what that means, girls. When your grandmother has a hunch, we usually get into some trouble," Uncle Jake teased.

"You mentioned Lilliputians back at Morgan's house," Granny said, after giving her son a wink. "We had to put an end to one of their crime sprees a while back. They're likely still in the town jail. Let's pay them a visit."

Sabrina and Daphne exchanged a look.

"The new sheriff is not exactly one of our biggest fans," Sabrina pointed out. Before Sheriff Nottingham was elected, the legendary villain of the Robin Hood story swore he'd devote every waking hour to locking up the Grimm family.

"Perhaps not." Granny Relda sighed. "But it can't hurt to ask."

"Actually, I think it could hurt a lot," Sabrina said with a shudder as she remembered the dagger the sheriff kept at his side.

When Sabrina got out of the car at the police station, she noticed that the bicycle store next door was closed. A big sign in the window said GOING OUT OF BUSINESS.

"I guess I can cross that off the list," Sabrina said. One of her birthday wishes was a bicycle.

"It appears times are tough all over," Granny Relda said as she pointed across the street. An antique shop and a florist were boarded up, each with signs hanging in the window that read SORRY, WE'RE CLOSED.

"That's strange," Uncle Jake said.

Entering the police station felt like stepping into the mouth of a lion, but luckily Nottingham was not in the lobby. In fact, the jail seemed deserted. Dusty Christmas decorations hung from the walls and a needleless pine tree was rotting in the corner. A few multicolored ornaments still clung to its lifeless limbs. These were decorations Sheriff Hamstead had set up back in December, and apparently Nottingham couldn't be bothered to put them away. It was just one example of the office's neglect. An inch of grime covered most surfaces, leaning towers of files spilled onto the filthy floor, and many of the desk chairs were broken and lying on the ground. The only new addition to the station was a full-length mirror leaning against a wall. Sabrina could just see Heart using it to admire her grotesque features.

"Hello!" Granny called out.

"He's gone," Sabrina said, her voice quaking with anxiety. "We should come back later."

Before anyone could take her advice, Sheriff Nottingham entered through a door at the far end of the room. He was a tall, angry man with long black hair that fell past his shoulders. A jagged scar ran from the bottom of one of his dark eyes to the corner of his lips. A goatee framed his mouth, cut into a point just under his chin.

"Well . . ." he seethed, "isn't this unexpected."

He limped over to the desk where the family was gathered. It was clear his leg was bothering him. According to the story, that old injury was thanks to one of Robin Hood's well-aimed arrows.

Granny plastered a fake smile on her face. "Sheriff Nottingham, it's very nice to see you. We haven't had the opportunity to talk since you were elected. My family and I wanted to say hello. I'm sure you're aware of our reputation as detectives. The previous administration found our unique talents very helpful, and I wanted to extend my hand with the hope we'll be able to work together for the good of the town."

"Extend your hand, woman, and you'll find me lopping it off with a sword," Nottingham threatened.

Uncle Jake stepped forward. "Threaten my mother again, pal, and you and I are going to have a very big problem."

The sheriff pulled his coat aside to reveal his shiny dagger. "Our problems have yet to begin."

Uncle Jake pulled his coat open to reveal hundreds of blinking rings, wands, and jewels. "If you're feeling froggy, Sheriff, I invite you to take a leap."

The two men stared each other down.

"Why are you here?" Nottingham demanded.

"We're investigating a series of robberies—" Granny Relda began.

"I haven't received any reports of robberies," Nottingham interrupted.

"I suppose you will once the citizens get to know you," Granny said. "But these are close friends, and we're trying to be helpful. Our investigation has led us here. We'd appreciate it if we could speak to the Lilliputians."

Nottingham laughed. "That's not possible. I released all the Everafter prisoners when I became sheriff."

"You did what?" Granny cried. "Some of those people were dangerous."

"Says you. This town is no longer your family's playground," Nottingham barked. "The Grimms have had their fun, and now it is over. In fact, you don't know just how over it is."

"What's that supposed to mean?" Uncle Jake asked, already reaching into his pockets for a weapon.

"I'm talking about the tax."

"The tax?" Sabrina asked.

"The property tax," Nottingham said with a wicked smile. "What? Didn't you get your letter?"

"What letter?"

Nottingham reached into the desk and pulled out a typed form. He threw it at Sabrina, who read aloud. "Property Tax Assessment. The town of Ferryport Landing has recently reassessed the value of your property, resulting in additional tax. Your estimated obligation is one hundred and fifty thousand dollars, due immediately."

"One hundred and fifty thousand dollars!" Granny groaned.

"Yes. Public services aren't free. There are schools and roads to maintain, and of course the police department. Everyone is going to have to pay their fair share."

"Even you?" Uncle Jake challenged.

"Me?" Nottingham laughed. "Of course not. I'm exempt. I'm an Everafter."

"You're only taxing the humans?" Granny Relda asked.

Uncle Jake growled. "You dirty, filthy, rotten—"

"Too many outsiders have come into this town, stealing our jobs and enjoying our hospitals and schools. Mayor Heart has decreed, and I wholeheartedly agree, that these undesirables have to go. Ferryport Landing is an Everafter town for Everafters!"

"What if people can't pay?" Granny Relda asked.

"That's unfortunate. I suppose we'll be forced to repossess their property."

"What does *repossess* mean?" Daphne whispered in Sabrina's ear.

"It means they can take our house and kick us out into the street," Sabrina replied, suddenly realizing why the bike store, florist, and antique shop were now closed.

Daphne turned to Nottingham. "Where will we go?"

"That's not the town's concern," Nottingham said, cracking his knuckles. "But don't worry. You have until Friday to pay your bill."

That's only two days away, Sabrina thought.

As the car cruised through the little town, Sabrina looked out the window at the passing houses. Everyone, it appeared, was having a yard sale, hawking their most prized possessions in hopes of paying the tax. She imagined Nottingham and Mayor Heart laughing at the troubles they had heaped on the human population of Ferryport Landing.

"This is nothing to worry about," Granny Relda said, though her expression didn't match her confident words. She kept reading and rereading the tax letter. "Nothing to worry about at all."

"Granny, do we have a hundred and fifty thousand dollars?" Daphne asked.

The old woman shook herself out of a daze. "I'm sorry, *liebling*. What did you say?"

"Do we have the money to pay the tax?"

The old woman flinched as if she'd been stung by an angry hornet. "We'll be fine, girls," she said, but Sabrina couldn't help feeling nervous. During her time in the orphanage and in dozens of foster homes, she'd honed the ability to recognize a lie. They were not going to be fine at all.

Later that evening, the girls dressed in their white martial arts robes, called *gis*. Sabrina helped Daphne wrap her yellow belt around her waist and then tied on her own white one. The colors represented levels of expertise; white was for beginners, yellow was more advanced. Once ready, the sisters met Puck in the hallway. Dressed in his usual jeans and green hooded sweatshirt, he had a big black scarf wrapped around his waist.

"I think you have to earn your black belt," Daphne said.

Puck rolled his eyes. "I'm already the best butt-kicker in this town. They don't even have a color for how good I am."

Sabrina unlocked the spare-room door that led to her sleeping parents and the magic mirror. She led Puck and Daphne through the reflection, where they found Mirror sitting in a chair enjoying a glass of wine and some expensive chocolates.

"Snow's down the hall," he said, pointing. "Have fun!"

The children found their teacher waiting for them near the rooms that held magical hats and Tooth Fairy teeth. Snow wore a white robe like the girls', but with a black belt wrapped around her waist.

"Hello, pupils," she said, bowing.

"Hello, sensei," Sabrina and Daphne said as they bowed back in respect. Puck, however, was picking his nose.

"Tonight we are going to continue working on blocking," Ms. White said.

Puck let out an exasperated groan. "Again! When are we going to learn to punch someone in the face?"

Snow White sighed. "Puck, I told you when you asked to join the girls' training sessions that karate is not about attack. It's about defense."

"Well, I'm starting my own martial art, then," he said. "It's called Puck-fu and there's only one move you need to learn—the knuckle sandwich."

"Well, I wish you luck with that, but Mrs. Grimm and I feel that the girls should learn to defend themselves against attackers," Ms. White said. "Now, everyone, let's get into our defensive stance."

Ms. White moved among the group, throwing training punches that allowed the children to block her attacks with ease. As the night rolled on, the attacks became more forceful. They worked on close-handed and open-handed blocks, how to step aside to avoid a punch, and how to use their own wrists to stop an assault. Ms. White was a patient teacher, but tonight she seemed a bit preoccupied. Sabrina wondered if she was thinking of Charming. Sabrina guessed his disappearance was weighing heavily on Snow's heart. Sabrina wanted to reach out to her, but what could she say? She certainly felt sympathy for Snow, but sometimes she wondered what the lovely teacher saw in the guy. Sure, he was handsome, but Charming could also be a jerk. He never did anything that wasn't in his own self-interest. He had helped the Grimms on a few occasions, but it always seemed to be motivated by a desire to impress Ms. White or advance his own career. Still, Sabrina felt she should say something.

"He'll turn up," she said softly, as she and Daphne walked Snow to the door.

Ms. White looked as if she were fighting back tears. "I hope so," she whispered, then told the children she would see them in a couple of days for their next class.

Puck was in the dining room wolfing down soup when the girls returned. There was a note on the table from Granny explaining that she had gone to bed early, that Mr. Canis was in his room, and that Uncle Jake was out for the night. She advised the children to have as much soup as they wanted and then to get to work researching tiny people and any small animals that might be capable of stealing magical items. Sabrina was dumbfounded. After their run-in with Nottingham and the news of the tax assessment, she wondered why the family was still bothering with the mystery. They had much bigger problems to deal with than a couple of stolen magical gizmos.

"She must be worried," Daphne said as she peered into the pot. "It's just chicken noodle. There's nothing purple or glowing in it at all."

Sabrina made a bowl for her sister and then did the same for herself. They sat with Puck, who, after several threats, surrendered a few of the fresh rolls he was hoarding.

"You better be nice to me," Puck said around a mouthful of soup. "When you two are homeless, you're going to want to live with me, and I won't let just anyone live in my forest!"

"Are we really going to be homeless?" Daphne asked.

"No!" Sabrina said.

"Don't lie to her," Puck said. "Things are bleak, marshmallow. If I were you, I'd eat as much of this soup as you can. Hoboes have to eat out of garbage cans and beg for crusts of bread in the street. This might be the last meal you get for a long time."

"I don't want to be a hobo," Daphne said, then turned to her sister. "What's a *hobo*?"

Sabrina ignored the question.

"Give me that roll, and I'll find you a nice warm refrigerator box to sleep in," Puck said.

"Daphne, don't listen to him," Sabrina said.

Daphne surrendered her roll to Puck anyway.

"We need to get to work," Sabrina said with a sigh.

"Well, that's my cue," Puck said as he pushed back from the table. He had once claimed he was allergic to books and often said people who tried to improve their minds were just admitting stupidity. He flew off to his room, leaving the girls alone.

Sabrina went to the bookshelves and searched the titles for anything on little thieves. She found books by Tiny Tim and Thumbelina, and one titled *Life Is Futile* by the Itsy Bitsy Spider. She scooped them all up, set them on the table, then went back to scan the collection of family journals. Every Grimm since Wilhelm and Jacob, the men who'd brought the Everafters to Ferryport Landing, had faithfully documented his or her experiences in the town. Each journal was packed with eyewitness accounts, and they frequently proved very helpful in solving cases.

For hours, Sabrina and Daphne pored over the old books. They read about the Mouse King, sorted through the various campaigns of an army of tin soldiers, and learned about the history of Lilliput. But they found nothing definitive, and soon they were at a dead end. It was very late, and they were very tired. Even Elvis was fast asleep under the table.

"I thought detective work was supposed to be exciting," Sabrina whined, closing the book that lay before her.

"I'm excited," Daphne said.

"You're always excited," Sabrina replied, resting her head on the dining-room table. "Granny has probably already solved this case and just won't tell us what she knows."

"We're training," Daphne reminded her. "She wants us to figure this out for ourselves."

"She wants to drive us crazy. This town is filled to the brim with sneaky animals and tiny people, not to mention witches who might be able to shrink themselves. How can we narrow it down?"

"We'll figure it out," Daphne said. "Remember, we're a great team."

Sabrina was exhausted, but she had to smile. "C'mon, Elvis, you've probably got to go out," Sabrina said, nudging the big dog as she got up from the table.

He nearly knocked Sabrina over as he charged for the door. "Don't go far," she shouted after him as he barreled out into the yard.

"I'm getting some water," she said to her sister, crossing back into the kitchen. "Want anything?"

Daphne shook her head, which was resting on a big book about a village in Oz whose citizens were made of jigsaw-puzzle pieces.

Sabrina took a glass from the cupboard and opened the

refrigerator. Inside, there were several containers of leftovers, a package of bologna, and a bowl with a little sign on it that read DANGER! SAUSAGES! KEEP AWAY FROM ELVIS AT ALL COSTS! She reached for the jug of water and poured some into her glass. She almost dropped both when she heard an angry bark.

She peered out of the kitchen window and saw Elvis growling at the edge of the woods. At first she assumed Puck was out there preparing some humiliating trap for her, but then she spotted the odd, swirling clouds hovering over the backyard. Elvis hated thunder and often hid under the girls' bed during particularly loud storms.

She turned to put the jug back in the refrigerator but spun back around to the window when she heard a loud cry. Uncle Jake was bolting through the yard. He looked panicked and afraid. Suddenly, there was a whipping sound, and he crashed to the ground. An arrow was stuck in his back.

4

SABRINA'S GLASS SHATTERED WHEN IT HIT THE kitchen floor. The crash snapped her out of her shock, and she sprang into action. She raced into the dining room, pulled Daphne from her chair, and shoved her under the table.

"What's wrong?" the little girl asked.

"Stay here!" she ordered, then ran for the front door, shouting for Granny and Mr. Canis. She dashed into the backyard where she found her uncle lying facedown in the snow. Sabrina gently turned him over, and he let out a groan.

"Uncle Jake!" she cried—though looking at him closely, she wasn't positive that he was her uncle. There was something different about his face. He had a beard and a large scar on his neck that looked as if a rope had been tied tightly around it. His hair was gray on the sides, and his eyes seemed dull. He was clearly in a great deal of pain.

"'Brina? You look so young."

"Granny and Mr. Canis are going to help you. They're on their way," Sabrina said through panicked sobs.

"You look just like you did when you were twelve."

He's raving from the pain, Sabrina thought to herself. *He needs a doctor right away.* "Someone help us!" she shouted, fighting to be heard over the rumbling storm. She climbed to her feet and turned to the house. "Help!"

Elvis added his baleful barks to her cries, and in no time, Granny and Mr. Canis were rushing out of the house.

"*Liebling*, what is the matter?" Granny asked, rushing to her side. She was in her nightgown and slippers and had a green mud mask on her face.

"It's Uncle Jake. He's been hurt," Sabrina cried, turning to the fallen man. But much to her surprise, he was gone. Bewildered, Sabrina scanned the edge of the woods, wondering if he had somehow crawled away, but that didn't seem possible. She had only taken her eyes off him for a second. She studied the yard, searching for a trail of his blood, but there was nothing. It was as if her uncle hadn't been there at all.

"But . . . he was right here on the ground. I saw him. I saw the arrow! He was dying."

Elvis rushed to the place where Uncle Jake had fallen. He sniffed the ground and whined.

"Child, you are mistaken," Canis said. "No one has been injured. I would smell the blood."

"You must have been having a bad dream," Granny said to her. "Your Opa Basil used to walk in his sleep, too."

"No! I saw him. He was right here. We have to look for him!" she cried.

Uncle Jake walked around from the front of the house. He was his normal, healthy self: no scar on his neck and no beard. "What's all the commotion?"

Sabrina suddenly felt woozy and hot. Her vision filled with little flashes of light. "You were hurt . . . " she started to say, but then everything went black.

When Sabrina awoke the next morning, she felt as if she had been asleep for a hundred years. She was groggy, and her legs felt as wobbly as cooked spaghetti when she descended the steps to join her family for breakfast. When she saw that Uncle Jake was working his way through a box of donuts, she began to believe that perhaps her grandmother was right. Maybe the entire incident had been a very vivid nightmare. She wondered what her grandmother had put in the soup.

"Feeling better?" Granny asked, entering the dining room with a tray of magenta-colored hash browns. The old woman scooped a spoonful onto everyone's plate and a second helping onto Puck's.

Elvis crouched under the table, licking Sabrina's feet. They locked eyes and, though she couldn't be certain, it seemed as if the dog might be trying to tell her that he, too, remembered the tragic event.

"I'm fine," Sabrina said, though her head felt full of sludge.

"We were worried. Was that the first time you've hallucinated?" Granny said.

"What does *hallucinate* mean?" Daphne asked.

"It's when you think you see something that isn't really there," Sabrina said.

"It usually means you've lost your marbles," Puck added.

"When a person hallucinates, they see and hear things that aren't there. It doesn't mean they've lost their marbles," Granny Relda corrected. "There are many reasons why it can happen— not enough sleep, for instance. Perhaps the training is becoming a little too much for you."

"Or she could have touched something bad at Baba Yaga's house," Uncle Jake said.

"A good point, Jacob," the old woman said. "We'll have to be more careful when we go back."

"Go back!" Sabrina exclaimed.

"Sabrina, of course we'll have to go back when we find Baba Yaga's wand," Granny said, kissing her on the forehead.

"I can't wait to go back," Puck said. "Baba Yaga is very punk rock."

"Children, I need you to hurry up and eat this morning. We've got another busy day ahead of us."

"Are we back on the case?" Daphne asked in between bites.

Granny nodded. "Of course—but first we have to pay our taxes."

The courthouse was a grand building with a dome and marble columns, just a few doors down from the police station. Outside, a huge crowd of people marched, carrying signs and shouting angrily.

"Looks like a protest," Sabrina said, noticing a sign with the word TAX painted on it with a big red slash through it.

Mr. Canis parked on the side of the road and waited for the car to stop backfiring. "Relda, I don't believe it would be wise for me to walk through that crowd in my current condition."

Granny agreed. "Yes, a seven-foot man with a tail might attract some attention. Stay here. We'll be back in a jiffy."

"Please be careful," he instructed.

As the Grimms eased their way through the angry mob, they passed people who seemed totally desperate. An elderly man grabbed Sabrina by the arm and pleaded, "They can't do this to us. We've got nowhere to go."

Frightened, Sabrina pulled away and caught up with her grandmother and sister. They entered the double doors of the courthouse and immediately spotted an armed guard who gave them directions to the tax assessor's office.

"Is there much of a line?" Granny asked the man.

The guard shook his head. "You're the first people I know of who have the money to pay."

At the end of a long narrow hallway, they came to a door with TAX ASSESSOR'S OFFICE stenciled on its window. A little red tag hanging from the doorknob read BE BACK IN 15 MINUTES.

"I guess we have to wait," Granny said.

Fifteen minutes turned into two and a half hours. Finally, a short, stocky woman approached from the other end of the hallway. As she came closer Sabrina recognized her as Mayor Heart, the former Queen of Hearts from Alice's famous adventures documented by Lewis Carroll. Sabrina thought the mayor looked like a demented beauty-pageant contestant. Her face was painted in bold, harsh colors—bloodred lips, dark purple eyeshadow, mahogany brown eyebrows, and a black hole of a beauty mark on her left cheek. She was wearing an elaborate crimson gown with little hearts sewn into it. She held an electronic megaphone in her hand. The protesters followed behind her, waving their tax-assessment letters in the air furiously. Mayor Heart seemed to be enjoying their frustration—or it could have been her obnoxious makeup that made her seem amused. Sabrina couldn't be sure.

"People, what's done is done," Mayor Heart announced through the entirely too loud megaphone. Her words echoed off

the walls, causing a high-pitched feedback that rang in everyone's ears. "The city needs the funds, and you're going to pay them or you're going to move."

"I'll get a lawyer!" one man threatened.

"Feel free," Heart said. "But I have a feeling any lawyer in this town is in the same boat as you. Now get lost, or I'll have the sheriff lock you all up."

"For what?" one man shouted. "It's still legal to protest in this country."

"Then I'll have you locked up for being ugly. Now scram!"

The people filed out slowly until the mayor and the Grimms were alone. Heart let out a little laugh when she noticed them. She unlocked the door to the tax assessor's office, snatching the note off the knob as she entered.

Granny Relda and the girls followed her and found themselves in a small, windowless office lined with big gray filing cabinets. Heart stepped behind a well-worn counter and set a bell on top of it.

"Good morning, Mayor Heart," Granny said as she stepped up to the counter.

The mayor said nothing. In fact, she opened up a drawer, took out a newspaper, and started reading the day's headlines.

"Hello?" Sabrina said.

Daphne tugged on her grandmother's sleeve and pointed to a sign on the wall. It read RING BELL FOR SERVICE.

Granny looked as if she might leap over the counter and strangle Mayor Heart, but instead she took a deep breath and lightly tapped the bell once. The mayor looked up from her paper and flashed the family a smile filled with crooked yellow teeth. "Next! How can I help you?"

"Mayor Heart, I didn't realize you were required to collect the taxes personally," Granny said.

"Oh, I'm not," the mayor said with a twisted giggle. "But this job is just too much fun to let someone else do it. I suppose you're here to see if you can talk your way out of your debt like all the other filthy humans?"

"Not at all," Granny said as she took a stack of money from her handbag. "I'm here to pay the bill."

The mayor's face turned bright red even through her white pancake makeup. She tried to speak but fell into a coughing fit for several moments before she managed to squeak out, "You what?"

"We'd like to pay our taxes. Is this the correct office?" Granny asked politely.

The mayor stammered and looked as if she might lapse into a fit. "Yes, it is."

"Very well," the old woman said as she placed two stacks of cash on the mayor's desk. "One hundred and fifty thousand dollars."

Ms. Heart reached underneath the desk and snatched her

megaphone. She bellowed into it, "NOTTINGHAM!" The feed-back rattled Sabrina's ears.

A moment later, the foul sheriff hobbled into the office. "I hear you, woman! If you haven't noticed, I'm a little busy. There's a mob outside, and some fool on Mount Taurus swears he's seen a dinosaur. Can you believe that? A dinosaur! I put him in a cell for being intoxicated."

"WHO CARES?" the mayor roared into her megaphone. "The Grimms have arrived to pay their taxes."

Nottingham laughed long and hard, but then realized his boss was not joking. He scowled and slammed his fist down on the counter, cursing and spitting in frustration.

"The two of you act as if you're disappointed that we can pay," Granny said, obviously enjoying the change in mood.

Nottingham snatched the money off the desk and flipped through it as if he suspected it were counterfeit.

"We're going to need a receipt," Granny said sweetly.

Mayor Heart snarled as she scribbled out a receipt. "This isn't over," Heart said, dangling the receipt just out of Granny Relda's reach.

"Oh, we never doubted that for a second," the old woman replied.

Ms. Heart lowered the receipt and Granny took it, placing it safely in her handbag. Then she took each of the girls by the hand and escorted them out of the office.

"Have a nice day," Daphne said as they exited.

Much to the satisfaction of Granny Relda, Sabrina heard the mayor and the sheriff groan in frustration as the door closed behind the Grimms. But when they stepped outside, they were met with throngs of desperate citizens. Granny's smile quickly faded.

"These poor people. If we had enough I'd give them all the money they need," she said.

They hadn't taken a single step away from the courthouse before Nottingham rushed out the doors, waving a paper over his head. "Oh, Mrs. Grimm . . ."

"Sheriff, is there a problem?" Granny asked.

"Indeed," Nottingham replied. "It appears we've miscalculated the tax on your property."

"Oh, a refund," Granny said, clapping her hands.

"Bah!" the man said with a sick laugh. "The assessment of your house failed to calculate the value of the land it is built on. You have nearly three acres of incredibly valuable property. I'm afraid we need to add to your tax liability."

"How much more?" Sabrina asked suspiciously.

"Oh, just another three hundred thousand dollars," the sheriff replied.

"That's outrageous!" Granny Relda cried.

"It is, isn't it?" Nottingham said as a sinister grin crept across his face. Sabrina couldn't help but stare at the horrible scar that ran down the man's face. She wondered if that was what made him so ugly, or if he had been grotesque before the knife had done its work.

"And when we pay this, what are you going to tax next? The air around the house? You're just trying to get rid of us!" Sabrina shouted.

"You're not as stupid as I was led to believe, girlie," the sheriff said. "By the way, the taxes are due on Friday."

When they got home, Granny Relda was dazed and distant, wandering from room to room and talking to herself in German. She made some peanut-butter-and-rose-petal sandwiches for the girls and Puck, then asked Uncle Jake and Mr. Canis for a moment of their time. The three adults went upstairs for some privacy.

"This is bad," Daphne said.

"Don't worry, marshmallow. You'll get used to the cold," Puck said as he slathered mustard all over his sandwich.

Sabrina flashed the boy a look that said *Shut your trap*.

Moments later, Uncle Jake returned. "Good news, girls. I'm going to help you with your case. Your grandmother is a little busy with the financials, but it's nothing to worry about."

"Granny said the same thing when we only owed a hundred and fifty thousand dollars," Daphne reminded him.

"It's all just details. Now, where are we on the case?"

"At a dead end," Sabrina reminded him.

"Any suspects?"

"Too many to count," Daphne said.

Uncle Jake scratched his head. "Well, let's review what we know so far. Both the victims are Everafters. Both were robbed of magical items. Whoever or whatever robbed them was pretty small, or had the ability to make themselves small. Anything else?"

Daphne spoke up. "The victims are both women."

"They're both witches," Sabrina added.

"They were both here the other night," Puck said without looking up from his fourth sandwich. Everyone turned to look at him. Sabrina was shocked that the boy fairy had even noticed.

"That's a good point, Puck," Uncle Jake said. "Both of the victims visited us two nights ago."

"Do you think there might be a connection?" Sabrina asked.

"Could be," Uncle Jake said. "Only one way to find out. We have to ask the others who came to the party. Maybe they've got something missing, too."

"There were a lot of guests. Who should we see first?" Daphne asked.

Uncle Jake grinned. "Let's go talk to Briar."

Sabrina rolled her eyes. "You just want to go see your crush."

Jake blushed and played dumb. "A good detective goes where the leads take him."

As they drove through the town, Uncle Jake chattered on about how pretty Briar Rose was, how smart Briar Rose was, how he hoped Briar Rose wasn't mixed up in the mystery. Puck threatened to leap from the car several times to put himself out of his misery, and Sabrina was considering joining him. After a while, even Daphne got tired of hearing Uncle Jake sing the princess's praises.

Luckily, Briar's place of business was not far from the Grimm house. Ms. Rose owned a quaint little coffee shop near the courthouse. It faced the Hudson River, not far from the train station and a tiny marina. Sacred Grounds, as it was called, was a favorite of the town's coffee fanatics. The chalkboard outside promised dozens of different coffees, from au laits and espressos to something called a café macchiato. It also advertised a variety of muffins, scones, cookies, and donuts. Every time Sabrina passed the shop, it was jam-packed with customers. Coffee seemed to have the same effect on adults as magic did on her. She remembered her own mother waiting in line for what seemed like an hour to buy a seven-dollar latte.

Once outside the store Uncle Jake ran his fingers through his hair, blew into his hand to make sure his breath was sweet, and straightened the collar of his shirt.

"How do I look?" he asked the children.

"Why do you care? She's just a girl," Puck said. "Girls are disgusting."

"You won't always feel like that," Uncle Jake said.

"Wanna bet?"

"You look mucho handsome-o," Daphne said with a wink.

Uncle Jake led everyone into the shop. It was packed wall-to-wall with people: chatting, working on laptops, and sipping from tall, frothy cups of coffee. There were several little tables scattered about and a bright glass case in the front was filled with pastries. There was also a long line of impatient, agitated people.

Sabrina spotted Briar Rose behind the counter. Even with her hair pulled back and an apron tied around her waist, she was a knockout. She worked the cash register, ringing up orders and keeping the line moving as quickly as possible, which wasn't easy. Most of the customers wanted coffees with ridiculously long names and detailed preparation instructions.

"I want a large decaf nonfat soy iced cappuccino with sugar-free hazelnut syrup."

"Give me a triple red eye with lactose-free milk and cane sugar."

"One extra-large chai latte with a dash of fresh cinnamon."

The family stood in line and slowly worked their way to the counter.

"Jacob," Ms. Rose said sweetly when it was their turn.

"Briar," he replied. "You look amazing."

The princess blushed. "You always say that."

"It's always true."

"Don't distract her," said a little old woman at the end of the line. "I need my caffeine, and I need it now!"

"Sorry, Mrs. Finnegan," the princess said. "It'll only take a second."

"C'mon, pal," a man shouted from the middle of the line. "We've been here a long time."

Sabrina cringed. "They're going to kill us all right here in the café."

"Briar, what is the holdup?" Mallobarb asked as she approached the counter, Buzzflower by her side. When the fairy godmothers spotted Uncle Jake, they scowled.

"Paying customers only," Buzzflower said angrily.

"Hello, ladies, we're happy to buy something," Uncle Jake said. "In fact, we haven't had lunch yet. We'll take four of those blueberry muffins, and I'll have a coffee."

"What kind of coffee?" Mallobarb snapped.

"What do you mean what kind? Coffee-coffee," he replied.

The line let out a collective groan, and Mrs. Finnegan could be heard muttering, "Amateurs."

"Get him the African blend," Briar said to her fairy godmothers.

They flashed Uncle Jake a suspicious look but rushed to fill the order. This gave Uncle Jake and Briar a rare moment together away from the disapproving eyes of her fairy chaperones.

"Any chance you could take a break?" Uncle Jake asked.

"NO!" everyone in the line shouted.

"We're in the middle of our lunchtime rush," Briar explained.

"Just a second?" Uncle Jake pleaded, flashing a handsome grin at the princess.

Briar Rose laughed and then took off her apron. "Ladies, I'll be right back," she called.

Those waiting in line were visibly enraged.

"People, please, try some decaf," Uncle Jake said. He opened the door wide for the children and Briar Rose.

"Sorry about that," Briar said once they were outside. "Coffee is addictive, and people get angry when they need their fix."

"I've gotten warmer receptions from banshees," Uncle Jake joked.

"At least Mallobarb and Buzzflower didn't try to turn you into a dung beetle this time," Briar pointed out.

"I told you I'd win them over."

Briar laughed. "I had a nice time last night."

"I'm still embarrassed about the meatball," Jake said, blushing.

"I had no idea they were so aerodynamic," Ms. Rose said with a giggle.

"I have to admit, I'm a bit of a klutz. If you keep seeing me, I'm going to ruin your entire wardrobe."

"Well, then you're lucky I like to shop," the princess said.

"Could someone please kill me?" Puck begged. "If I have to hear one more word of this mushy love story, I'm going to throw myself off a bridge."

"Uh, I hate to admit it, but Puck's right. Aren't we supposed to be solving a mystery here?" Sabrina said.

"Well, hello!" a voice called from behind them. The group turned to find Tom Baxter crossing the street. He was with three young men, all wearing glasses and sweaters. Each wore a button that read I CALLED THE DR. CINDY SHOW. "Nice to see you again," the old man said with a smile.

"Nice to see you, too," Daphne said. "Where's Dr. Cindy?"

Tom pointed across the street at a tall building with a huge metal tower on its roof. It was the offices of Ferryport Landing's radio station, WFPR.

"She's busy preparing for tonight's show. It takes an awful lot of planning," Tom said. "But I'm being rude. Folks, these are some of my colleagues. Malcolm is our show's producer, Alexander is our sound engineer, and Bradford fields phone calls. They also help me cross the street from time to time."

"It's very nice to meet you. I never miss a show," Puck said, shaking their hands.

Sabrina turned, half expecting to find the boy was teasing the men, but he was dead serious.

"What?" Puck asked defensively. "You should hear the people that call Dr. Cindy. All of them are sad, depressed, and lonely. It's one of the funniest shows on the radio."

Malcolm frowned. "Well, we better grab our coffee and get back."

"He's right," Tom said with a laugh. "Cindy can be a real bear when she doesn't get her cappuccino."

The Grimms said their good-byes, and Tom and his coworkers entered the coffee shop just as Ms. White approached.

"Oh, good, Snow, I'm glad you're here. A few people who came to our party have since had some things stolen from their homes," Uncle Jake said. "I don't want to pry, but if you have something missing that might be a little magical, we'd like to know. Briar, have you or your fairy godmothers been robbed?"

"Mallobarb and Buzzflower don't let their magic wands out of sight, and all I have at home are a handful of magic seeds. Everything is accounted for, as far as I know."

"Perhaps I could come over some evening and help you double check," Uncle Jake said with a grin.

Briar's cheeks turned pink, but she didn't lose her smile.

"Jacob Grimm, you never change," Ms. White said with a laugh. "As for me, I think everything is fine. Maybe you should ask Frau Pfefferkuchenhaus, too. Her office is right next door."

"Good idea. Kids, go do that," Uncle Jake said, winking at

them. Sabrina didn't have to be a mind reader to know he was trying to get a little alone time with his princess.

"Sure, we'll go take a look," Sabrina said, pulling her sister and Puck along. They walked next door and spotted a sign on the building that read DR. F. PFEFFERKUCHENHAUS—DENTIST. On the front door was a painting of several happy children with enormous, toothy smiles and a speech balloon that read, EVERY-ONE SMILES FOR DR. P!

"What's a dentist?" Puck asked.

Sabrina cringed, imagining the four-thousand-year-old cavities the boy must have.

The lobby was neat and clean, with paintings of dancing teeth all over the walls. A thin receptionist with eyeglasses that made her look like an owl sat at the desk filling out paperwork.

"Welcome to Dr. P's," she said, looking up. Her glasses were so thick, Sabrina wondered if the woman might be able to see through her. "Do you have an appointment?"

"No, actually, we were hoping we could talk to the doctor. Tell her that Sabrina and Daphne Grimm are here. She'll see us."

The receptionist picked up the phone and tapped a few buttons. "Dr. P, I'm sorry, I know you're with a patient. There are three children out here who say they know you. They say their name is Grimm . . . really? Of course."

She hung up the phone. "She'll see you."

She led the group along a hallway lined with several open doors. Inside, Sabrina could see patients getting their teeth cleaned. The high-pitched squeal of drills filled the air. Somewhere, a man let out a painful groan.

"Is this a torture chamber?" Puck asked eagerly.

"This is a dental office," the receptionist explained. "People come here to get a healthy smile."

There was another groan.

Puck laughed. "Sure! That guy sounds like he's smiling, all right! Are you hiring?"

The receptionist ushered them into a room where they found the notorious witch probing the teeth of a very nervous man. Sabrina was familiar with the story Hansel and Gretel and knew the witch's reputation, but she also knew the old woman occasionally came to the family's assistance. Was she one of the good guys or a villain? In Ferryport Landing it was difficult to tell. Sabrina had certainly never suspected that the witch's day job was dentistry. Hadn't she once lived in a house made out of candy?

"Mr. Easy, can you feel that?" she asked her patient. He had a suction tube in his mouth and Dr. P's fingers on his tongue.

The man said no, though with some difficulty.

"What about that?"

"No!"

"Good, and what about this one here?"

The man cried out in agony.

"OK, looks like you need some more gas," the witch said, covering Mr. Easy's mouth and nose with a mask connected to a tank by a long tube. The man took several deep breaths, and his tense hands relaxed their grip on the sides of his chair.

"Hello, Grimms. What can I do for you?" the witch said. "I'm having a special on root canals."

"We'll pass," Sabrina said. "We're investigating a series of crimes. Maybe you've heard about Morgan le Fay and Baba Yaga's problems?"

"Indeed I have," the witch said. "Let me finish up with Mr. Easy here, and I'll be right with you."

Dr. P picked up a tiny drill and turned it on. It whined loudly as she went to work on the poor man's teeth. The gas she gave him must have been wonderfully strong, as he barely even reacted.

Puck pushed his way in front of the girls to get a better view. "I think I know what I want to be when I grow up," he said.

"Oh, there's lots of money in dentistry," the witch said over the noise. "People just can't get enough sugary sweets, and they rarely floss. I've got appointments backed up for months."

"You mean people pay you to do this to them? I thought you captured this guy and brought him here against his will," Puck said. "How do I become a dentist?"

"You have to go to school," Sabrina said, hoping the thought of an education might deter Puck's sudden career choice.

"You do?" the witch asked, eyeing Sabrina. "I didn't know that."

Mr. Easy mumbled something about seeing her dentistry license.

"What's that? You need more gas?" the witch said, shoving the mask back onto the man's face. Seconds later, he was, once again, incoherent. "I used to sell candy out of this place, but the story hurt business so badly I couldn't even drag kids in here. And, believe me, I tried."

"The story about Hansel and Gretel?" Daphne asked.

The witch nodded.

"Are you surprised?" Sabrina asked.

"You did try to eat them," Daphne added.

"Oh, I did not!" the witch said, suddenly jerking up and making a terrible cracking sound in Mr. Easy's mouth. "I was just trying to scare the little brats."

"That's not what I read," Sabrina said. Hansel and Gretel wandered into the woods and found a house made out of candy and gingerbread. The witch captured the children and tried to fatten them up so she could devour them.

"Well, you shouldn't believe everything you read." Dr. P snapped. "First of all, those kids were out of control, wandering around in the woods, making all kinds of racket. I mean, what kind of parent lets their kids play in a forest? Really!

"Second, they were eating my house," the witch continued as she went back to work on Mr. Easy's teeth. "The boy was outside gnawing on the fence, the girl was licking the shutters. I called the police, and you know what they told me? That if I was going to live in a house made of candy, I should expect children to come along and eat it. Is that what I was paying taxes for? No! So I took the law into my own hands."

"You put them in a cage!" Sabrina said.

Puck laughed. "That's so awesome."

"Only for half an hour!" the witch argued. "Plus, I fed them, and trust me, it was the only decent meal those kids had had in a long time. Their mother never saw a carbohydrate she didn't love, and they were really packing on the pounds. I gave them a salad. They had no idea what it was—apparently, they'd never eaten anything green that wasn't covered in cheese sauce! I let them go after dinner, and before I knew it I was 'a cannibal.' I tell you, the only thing bigger than their waistbands was their imagination."

The witch set her tools down and took off her latex gloves. "Mr. Easy, I've got good news and bad news," she said to her patient, who gazed at her dreamily. "The good news is we're going to be able to save the bicuspid. The bad news: All the other teeth are going to have to come out."

"What?" Mr. Easy cried.

"You need more gas," said Frau Pfefferkuchenhaus, putting the mask back over his face. "Just breathe deeply."

Mr. Easy's head wobbled, and a line of drool dribbled down his chin. "Mughadinkalbeettershpliem," he mumbled.

The witch got up from her chair and led the children out into the hallway.

"We didn't mean to bother you, but we were wondering if anything's been stolen from you. Say, something magical?" Sabrina asked.

The ancient witch shuffled uncomfortably and nodded. "I had a vial of water from the Fountain of Youth. It's gone."

"Why didn't you ever use it?" Puck asked rudely.

"First of all, I'm comfortable with my age. After all, two thousand and fifty is the new thirty! Besides, the water doesn't make you young," she explained. "It just stops you from getting older. I'm an Everafter, so it's not going to work on me anyway. I thought I might make a little extra cash someday selling it to a human. But when I came in this morning, it had been taken. Someone stole it right out of my locker."

"Could we take a look at the locker?" Sabrina asked.

The witch led them into a small room where they found a table, some jackets hanging on the wall, and a row of lockers. One was missing a door. It had been ripped off its hinges and now leaned against the wall.

"Wow, that can't have been easy," Daphne said.

"Whoever did it is very strong," the witch said.

Sabrina closely examined the warped locker door. "It's bent outward, like it was pushed from the inside. If someone ripped it off from the outside, the bend would be going in the opposite direction."

"But how did they get inside the locker?"

Sabrina looked inside and spotted the witch's handbag. There was a small hole in the fabric on the side, identical in size to the one in Morgan le Fay's purse. She showed her discovery to Daphne and the girls shared a knowing look.

"So you think whatever stole my vial was inside this locker?" the witch said.

Sabrina nodded.

"Can you get the vial back for me?" the old witch asked. "It's sort of my retirement plan."

"We'll try," Sabrina said. "But maybe you can answer one more question. So far, Merlin's wand, the Wonder Clock, and your Fountain of Youth water are missing. Why would someone want those three things?"

"I honestly can't say. Aside from the wand, the others are sort of low-grade magic. I can't imagine how much trouble they could cause unless . . . well, maybe someone is trying to combine their magic to make something new."

"Something new?" Sabrina asked. "You can do that?"

"Sure. If you combine the properties of different magical items, you can create a brand-new enchantment, though you'd have to be a pretty good sorcerer to make sure it didn't blow up in your face. Combining magical items can have unpredictable side-effects."

Just then, the receptionist entered the room. "I'm sorry, Doctor, but Mr. Easy is trying to escape."

"Give him some more gas and sit on him if you have to. I'll be right there," the witch said. "Listen, I've got to run. Teeth don't pull themselves. If you find anything, let me know."

The witch darted down the hallway, leaving them alone.

"So, what have we learned?" Daphne asked, doing a funny impression of their grandmother's German accent.

"I learned that you need no formal training to be a dentist!" Puck said.

"I learned the Lilliputians and the Mouse King are no longer suspects," Sabrina said. "I don't think they're strong enough to rip a steel locker door off its hinges."

The children found their uncle and Briar Rose exactly where they'd left them in front of the café, only this time they were holding hands. Ms. White was long gone.

"Any luck?" Uncle Jake asked when he noticed them.

"A little, but we need to get home," Sabrina said.

The adults both frowned, but Uncle Jake reluctantly pulled away from the princess, kissing her hand. "Until we meet again."

"OK, enough!" Puck cried. "If I have to, I'll turn a hose on you both."

Uncle Jake scowled. But before he could complain about the

children ruining his romantic moment, there was a terrible rumble, as if an earthquake were building beneath the streets. The tremors continued to grow in power, and then an explosion rattled the windows of the coffee shop. When the Grimms turned to face the source of the blast, they found Baba Yaga and her house stomping through town. Worse, the old crone was shooting fireballs from one of her magic wands.

5

I WANT MY PROPERTY!" THE WITCH SHRIEKED.

"Briar, you should get to safety," Uncle Jake said as he began digging in his pockets.

"What about you?" Briar cried.

"Don't worry, I'm a Grimm. This is what we do."

Sabrina watched the princess run and wondered if she and her family should do the same. Baba Yaga was tearing through town, blasting one building after another. She screeched at the top of her lungs to be heard over her home's rumbling footsteps.

"Look at all the chaos she's creating!" Puck shouted. "She's like my soulmate!"

The witch's house came to a stop outside the coffee shop and then bent down so that Uncle Jake's face and Baba Yaga's were just a few feet apart. The witch breathed heavily and growled like an angry dog.

"Let me guess. You haven't had your coffee," Uncle Jake said.

"I'll run in and get you one, and you'll feel better right away. How about a muffin to go with it? I hear the blueberry is to die for."

Baba Yaga shrieked again. "Have you got my wand, Grimm?"

Uncle Jake shook his head.

"Then I will find it myself, and woe to anyone who stands in my way. Step aside, boy."

"No can do. You see, this store is owned by a very special princess. I can't let you burn it down. But if you have to destroy something, the tax assessor's office is just up the block."

Baba Yaga lifted her hands and a ball of fire appeared in them. It grew until it was as big as a beach ball, and she wound up like a major-league pitcher.

"Uh-oh," Uncle Jake said. He took a small green amulet from his pocket and held it above his head. A light shot out of it, rising high into the air, then arcing down and slamming into the ground as if it were one solid, heavy mass. A tremor rose up like a mighty ocean wave, buckling the concrete and toppling Baba Yaga's house. The hut's legs flailed as it tried desperately to right itself. It wasn't long before the shack was back on its feet.

"What now?" Sabrina asked.

"What do you mean, 'What now?'" Uncle Jake said. "That should have taken care of her."

Then something happened that surprised even Baba Yaga—a thick black storm cloud appeared overhead. The wind swirled viciously, ripping the awning off the front of Sacred Grounds. With a flash of lightning and a crash of thunder, a dozen men in loincloths and painted faces appeared out of thin air. They were bare-chested and shoeless. A few held tomahawks in their hands, some had long spears, and others had bows and arrows. To Sabrina, they looked as if they had stepped out of the Native American exhibit at the American Museum of Natural History.

The men scanned the area, then trained their weapons on Baba Yaga and shouted to one another in a language Sabrina couldn't understand. Suddenly, they charged, attacking with ferocious might. Their spears stabbed at the house's legs, causing it to hop up and down. Sabrina watched as Baba Yaga tried to cast a spell against the men, but with the house rocking back and forth so much, she couldn't keep her balance. Some of the men launched their arrows directly at her, and the witch had to dive out of the way to avoid being hit. A few of the arrows stuck into the sides of the house, and the shack writhed in pain. Other men climbed its legs, taking advantage of the confusion, and smashed their tomahawks into the walls. Pieces of wood splintered and fell to the ground.

"Nice work," Daphne said to their uncle.

"Uh, I didn't do this," Uncle Jake said, completely flabbergasted as he looked down at the little amulet. "At least, I don't think I did."

Nottingham raced down the street with his dagger in hand. He came to a screeching halt when he spotted the scene in the middle of the road.

"Your little butter knife isn't going to do much," Uncle Jake said to the sheriff as he pointed at the rows of burning buildings. "We've got a bigger problem now, anyway. Call the fire department."

Nottingham's face turned red. "That's not possible."

"What? Why?" Sabrina demanded.

"The fire department was disbanded. The mayor had to make cuts, and there wasn't room for them in the budget. Charming left us with quite a debt, you know."

"What are we going to do?" Sabrina yelled as the strange men fired another volley of arrows at Baba Yaga's shack.

"I'll handle it," Uncle Jake said, fumbling around in his pockets. He took out a golden ring, placed it on his hand, then rubbed it against his sleeve to shine the emerald at its center. He whispered something into it, and it lit up like a brilliant firecracker. A moment later, the sky emptied buckets of water on everything. There was so much rain that Sabrina could barely see Daphne well enough to grab her hand. The rain swallowed up the flames, saving the town from imminent destruction.

When the rain slowed, Sabrina realized that the bizarre

thunderstorm had also vanished, along with the men and their weapons. All that was left was a bewildered Baba Yaga and her damaged home.

"This isn't over!" Baba Yaga cried as she craned her head out of one of her smashed windows. "I'll be back!"

The house turned and stomped back down the street the way it had come.

"Native Americans?" Granny Relda asked.

Uncle Jake nodded. "They looked like Lenapes from colonial times, if I remember history class correctly."

Mr. Canis groaned. "And where are they now?"

"They vanished the way they came—into thin air," Uncle Jake said, examining his amulet.

"I wonder how Mayor Heart will clean up that mess without a coven of witches on her side. The Three used to take care of magical problems when Charming was in charge," Granny said.

"There is no one to hide it from now. Almost all the humans have left town," Mr. Canis replied. "We still have to deal with Baba Yaga. The truth is, someone has to keep an eye on her. I could track her and make sure she doesn't get too close to the town."

"No, I need you to look after the girls," Granny Relda said. "Jacob will take care of Baba Yaga."

"Me?" Uncle Jake cried. "You know she threatened to eat me once, right?"

"You have the most experience with magical attacks," Granny said.

"I'll help you," Puck said. "She fascinates me."

"What about the case?" Daphne asked.

Granny shook her head. "*Liebling*, I'm afraid we're going to have to put detective work on hold. There are too many emergencies to deal with, and we can't be everywhere at once."

"But—" Sabrina started, but her grandmother threw up her hands.

"It's settled. Now, I have to get ready. Ms. White has offered to take me to the bank. I'm applying for a loan to pay our taxes."

Everyone darted off in his or her own direction, leaving Sabrina and Daphne alone with Mr. Canis, who didn't look at all happy to be stuck watching the girls.

"So . . ." Sabrina said as she eyed the old man. His upper fangs had started to grow past his lips.

"So," he huffed.

"You're babysitting us, huh?"

Mr. Canis raised his eyebrows, acknowledging his new role.

"Want to play a game?" Daphne asked. "We've got Candy Land."

Mr. Canis shifted uncomfortably.

"No!" Daphne cried as she jumped to her feet. "I know what we can do. We can play dress-up!"

Sabrina couldn't help but laugh.

"Perhaps we should continue with your tracking lessons," Mr. Canis said to the girls. "Put on your boots. We still have a few hours of daylight left."

Mr. Canis led them around the back of the house and deep into the woods. The ground was muddy and there was a chill in the air, but some little buds were sprouting on tree limbs in defiance. Sabrina wondered what the forest would look like when it was fresh and alive rather than dead and creepy.

They climbed along a small ravine and up a hill littered with sharp stones, then down into a gulch. A tiny creek trickled along with shards of ice floating on its surface.

"Are we going to lose the house?" Daphne asked the old man.

"Your grandmother is a resourceful woman," Mr. Canis replied.

"That's not an answer," Sabrina said. She didn't want to anger the old man, which had become increasingly easy to do, but she needed him to be honest with them.

"She will not let you down, girls. In the time I have known her, she has never failed. I trust her. You should as well."

"Three hundred thousand dollars is a lot of money," Sabrina pointed out.

"Yes, it is," the old man agreed. "Fortunately, this situation will benefit you in your training. Stress is an enemy. It confuses us and makes us question ourselves. The calm, rational mind is the one that finds answers even in difficult times. Remember, you will not always have the carefree lives of children, but you will always be Grimms, and you will have to find ways to set aside your personal concerns."

"So you want us to forget about the tax bill?" Daphne said.

"The three-hundred-thousand-dollar tax bill?" Sabrina added.

Mr. Canis took an impatient breath. "Close your eyes."

The girls did as they were told.

"In the past we have tracked deer and rabbits, as well as the family dog. You've learned to follow and recognize the prints of many wild animals. Today, you will follow the prints of the most dangerous animal of all—me. I will hide from you in this forest, and you will have to use the skills I have taught you to find me. Your grandmother has become a well-practiced tracker, and she uses her talents quite frequently. Remember—use your senses. Learn to trust what you see, smell, hear, and feel. Work together, and you two should have no problem locating me."

"I've got a question," Daphne said.

There was no response.

"Mr. Canis?"

Sabrina opened her eyes. The old man was gone. She nudged Daphne softly, and the little girl looked around.

"Well, that was mucho rude-o," Daphne complained.

Sabrina scanned the dense woods. Canis was nowhere in sight, but he had left a trail in the snow. Following it wouldn't be too difficult—after all, in his semi-altered form Mr. Canis wore size-twenty-two shoes.

The girls followed the huge footprints through some heavy brush. The old man's path showed that he had run in one direction and then cut back in the other, obviously trying to confuse them.

"Are we really going to have to live in a refrigerator box like Puck said?" Daphne asked. "I don't think we'll all fit in a refrigerator box. Mr. Canis won't for sure, and what about Elvis? I guess we could get a washing machine box for him. We could even decorate it and cut out some windows."

The little girl rambled on, describing how, with a little creativity, they could turn an old cardboard box into a two-story colonial, while Sabrina led her along Mr. Canis's trail. It took them up a steep slope, but they found a couple of branches that doubled as walking sticks to help with the climb. At the crest of the hill they found more trees, but Mr. Canis's footprints had disappeared.

"Where did he go?" Daphne asked.

"Maybe he's soaking in our cardboard-box Jacuzzi," Sabrina replied.

"OK, fine, I'll concentrate," Daphne grumbled.

Sabrina scanned the area but saw nothing. *He couldn't have just vanished into thin air, but . . .*

"Look!" Sabrina said, pointing up at the trees. She saw dozens of limbs splintered and broken, with fresh yellow wood erupting from the rich brown bark. "He jumped up there and grabbed those branches. They snapped when he swung to the next tree."

"I thought he was a wolf, not a monkey."

Sabrina scanned the next tree and saw a similar broken limb. "Then he swung over there."

"You're mucho excellent-o at tracking."

Sabrina swelled with pride. Her sister was right. She was good at tracking. "Thanks," Sabrina said as she pointed toward a row of trees. "He went that way."

The girls held hands and continued through the woods. It dawned on Sabrina that this was what Puck must have done when he was stalking them during escape training. He used the environment against the girls, finding the little clues their feet and bodies left behind.

It wasn't long before they found another set of Mr. Canis's footprints. It led them to a churning brook.

"What now?"

"Close your eyes," Sabrina told her sister. "He told us to use all our senses."

She stood quietly, trying to sort through the noises around her:

MAGIC AND OTHER MISDEMEANORS

the bubbling water, the creaky branches swaying in the breeze, a bird chirping high in the trees. And then she heard it: A twig snapped in the brush nearby.

"He's in there," Sabrina said, pulling her sister along. They pushed through the bushes, even getting on their hands and knees to crawl. It wasn't easy, and the girls were filthy, but that was the least of their worries. Without warning, the gray sky had suddenly filled with a dark, swirling storm. A crack of thunder shook the earth, and bolts of lightning lit up the sky. It looked just like the storm during Baba Yaga's attack, and the one on the night Sabrina had imagined Uncle Jake's death.

"I think we should head back," Sabrina said. "That storm looks ugly."

"Mr. Canis!" Daphne shouted. "We're going home!"

"Can you hear us, Mr. Canis?" Sabrina yelled.

"I don't know if he can hear you," a growling voice said from within the bushes, "but I certainly can."

Sabrina studied the brush, trying to find the source of the familiar yet menacing voice. Rough laughter echoed around the girls on all sides.

When Sabrina finally spotted a pair of eyes peering back at her, a monstrous figure stepped forward, uprooting a tree that was in its way. When the creature was out in the open, Sabrina nearly screamed. Standing before her was a wolf as big as a grizzly bear,

113

standing on its two hind legs. It snarled at the girls as it studied them curiously.

"The Wolf," Daphne gasped.

Sabrina's mind was reeling. What had happened to cause Mr. Canis to totally lose control of himself? Why had he let the Big Bad Wolf out?

The Wolf stomped forward, shoving its snout into Daphne's face and growling.

"Don't try to run, girlie!" the Wolf snarled as he snatched her by her coat and lifted her off the ground. "You'll just build up my appetite."

Sabrina was terrified, but she couldn't let her sister get hurt. She rushed at the Wolf with her fists clenched. She was met with a painful backhand that sent her slamming into the ground. Her shoulder collided hard with a stone. Her arm didn't feel broken, but the pain was excruciating. She forced herself to stand.

The Wolf is bigger and stronger than me, but I have to do something, she thought to herself. She spotted a sharp black rock on the ground, snatched it up, aimed, and flung it as hard as she could. It hit the Wolf and bounced off his chest as if it were no bigger than a peanut.

"Was that supposed to hurt?" He laughed.

"No!" a voice called from behind Sabrina. "But I bet this will!"

A flaming rocket blasted past Sabrina and hit the Wolf squarely in the chest. He howled and fell backward, releasing Daphne, who tumbled to the ground. Sabrina rushed to her sister's side and dragged her away, then turned to find out who had saved them.

Two women stood behind her. One was tall with long blond hair; she had a deadly looking sword in her hands and an array of weapons strapped around her waist and legs, including daggers, grenades, and a whip. The other woman had dark brown hair and wore a long trench coat with hundreds of extra pockets sewn into it, just like Uncle Jake's coat. The brown-haired woman was also wearing several necklaces and jeweled rings, one of which was glowing. Her expression was stern and serious. She was beautiful, but her face was marred by a horrible scar.

"You're not going to touch them, mutt," the blond woman said, waving her sword in the air.

"Or someone is going to get fixed," the woman in the coat added.

The Wolf clambered to his feet and eyed the women. "Back off. These are my kills!"

"You back off, or I'll take your other eye," the woman with the sword threatened. It was then that Sabrina noticed that the Wolf's left eye was white with blindness and framed by an ugly scar.

The monster growled and charged the blond woman. She swung her sword and hit the beast in the arm. The Wolf shrieked

and swung his paw at her, hitting her so hard she slammed against a tree. The brunette rubbed the glowing ring against her jacket, and another flare rocketed at the monster. The Wolf leaped out of the way, dodging the blast.

The woman with the sword quickly recovered. With the Wolf confused, she climbed up onto his enormous back. Raising her sword high over his head, she brought the hilt down hard between his eyes. He staggered, dazed. "He's all yours, sister," she shouted to her companion.

The dark-haired woman pulled a wand from inside her coat. She flicked her wrist and said, "Gimme some chains." A ray of light shot out of the wand's tip, and a stream of particles formed a chain so thick it looked as if it could tie down a battleship. The woman's aim was perfect; the chains wove around the Wolf, binding him tightly. He struggled, snarling and snapping at the women, but he was helpless.

"Who are they?" Daphne whispered to her sister.

Sabrina wracked her brain for any reference to a couple of tough chicks who could take down the Big Bad Wolf. She'd never read anything in the family journals about them. "I was hoping you would know."

The blond woman turned to Sabrina and studied her closely. Suddenly her confident face paled, as if she had just seen a ghost. "It can't be . . ." she began, but she didn't get to finish. The Wolf broke free with a powerful shrug. He pounced, slamming into the women and knocking them both to the ground.

"I've been waiting a long time for this meal," the Wolf said, licking his huge jaws.

"Nuh-uh-uh," said a voice from above them. It was deep but had a playful, boyish quality. Sabrina looked up to find a man with golden hair descending from the trees. On his back was a pair of huge wings. "I hate it when people threaten my family. It's so . . . well, rude."

He shot an arrow from the crossbow in his hands. It hit the Wolf in the leg, and the monster bellowed in pain, crashing to the ground. The fairy then morphed into a saber-toothed tiger and charged. He sank his heavy fangs into the monster's back, and the Wolf shrieked.

"We need to go get help," Sabrina said, snatching Daphne by the sleeve and pulling her into the woods, leaving the battle behind.

"But the house is back the other way," Daphne cried.

"We're not going to the house," Sabrina said. "Granny's at the bank, and so is our secret weapon."

6

THE GIRLS HURRIED THROUGH THE WOODS, clambering over rocks and around trees until they finally found a road. Daphne pulled away to catch her breath.

"We can't just leave them back there. He'll kill them," Daphne argued.

"I think the three of them can defend themselves," Sabrina said, scanning the edge of the forest in case the Wolf had indeed slaughtered the odd trio and was now on their trail. "Besides, we're just a couple of kids. We need help if we're going to try to stop Mr. Canis."

"What kind of help?"

"You remember the key that Mr. Hamstead gave us before we left New York City?"

Daphne pulled a necklace out from under her shirt. Dangling from it was a small silver key with several numbers engraved on its side. "This?"

Sabrina nodded. "He told us to use it if Mr. Canis ever lost control of the Wolf. It opens a safe-deposit box. There's a weapon inside that can stop the Wolf in his tracks."

Daphne looked down at the silver key. "What's a safe-deposit box?"

"It's like a safe. You put your valuables in it. They keep them at the bank."

"That's where Granny is," Daphne pointed out.

"I know. She can help us, too. But we have to hurry."

Unfortunately, the road they found themselves on was the long way to town, and it took several hours of walking before they came across any hint of civilization. The first thing they recognized was Old MacDonald's farm, from the famous nursery rhyme. But as they approached, they were shocked to see that the farm looked abandoned. The fields were overgrown with weeds, the barns were falling down on themselves, and the cattle pens and livestock enclosures were empty. As they got closer they also noticed that the farmer's house had been destroyed by a terrible fire. Oddly, the destruction appeared to have occurred long ago.

"What happened?" Daphne said, asking the question Sabrina had knocking around in her own head.

"I don't know," Sabrina said. "Did Granny mention this to us?"

Daphne shook her head.

"C'mon," Sabrina said. "We can't hang around here all day. I think we've got another half an hour of walking before we even get to Main Street."

The girls soon came across the rusty railroad tracks that ran along the Hudson River and led to the train station at the center of town. As they walked along the tracks, they encountered more surprising scenes. The stern of an enormous sunken ship was sticking out of the river. Several broken-down cars lined the grassy beach. When they finally stepped into town, they noticed a sign above the train station. It had once read WELCOME TO FERRY-PORT LANDING, but someone had vandalized it. The sign now read BEWARE! YOU ARE NOW ENTERING FAIRYPORT LANDING!

Just as shocking was the state of the town itself. The shops were abandoned, their doors torn away and windows broken. Many were in flames, their alarms unanswered. The streets were completely deserted.

"This is going to take an awful lot of forgetful dust," Daphne said as she gaped at all the destruction.

Sabrina couldn't believe what she was seeing. "I guess Uncle Jake isn't doing such a good job of keeping Baba Yaga in check."

When they came upon the bank, they were stunned to find the building was nothing but cinders. Everything inside it was burned to a black ash, including the tellers' windows, the ATM, and most importantly, the safe-deposit boxes. There was nothing left.

"Granny!" Daphne cried, nearly in hysterics.

Sabrina reached down and scooped up a handful of ash. It was cool to the touch.

"Daphne, this happened a long time ago," Sabrina said, trying to reassure her sister while deciphering the puzzle before her. "If the bank burned down this morning, why is the ash cold? Something's wrong. This must be another hallucination."

"Well, I'm having one, too," Daphne said. "How is that possible?"

Before Sabrina could answer, the street went dark, as if something had suddenly blocked out the sun. Sabrina watched as a vast shadow covered the street and then zipped away. The sunshine returned as quickly as it had disappeared.

"Uh, what was that?" Daphne asked nervously.

A powerful roar rattled Sabrina's ears as well as a loose pane of glass in the window of Dr. P's abandoned dentist office. The glass fell from its frame and shattered on the pavement. Sabrina continued studying the sky. She spotted something far off. At first it was tiny—no bigger than a bird—but as it approached, she could see that it was actually enormous and incredibly fast. It had bright red wings, which spanned the width of a football field and supported a huge, reptilian body covered in scales. Its long tail slashed through the air. The creature's neck was snakelike, and its mouth was filled with enormous teeth. Sabrina had once seen a movie about a kid who had one as a pet, but this thing was no pet.

"Sabrina, is that what I think it is?" Daphne shouted.

Sabrina was struck speechless but she knew the truth. It was a dragon.

"Run!" Sabrina yelled, grabbing her sister's hand. Together they sped down the street, dodging potholes and burned-out cars. The dragon swooped down and landed in their path. It crouched down, almost like a cat, and sniffed the air around them. Its breath smelled of sulfur fumes.

The creature roared again, and a blast of blisteringly hot air danced across Sabrina's skin. Luckily the beast was too far away to burn them.

"Heads up, kiddies!" said a voice from above. Sabrina looked to the sky, sure the voice belonged to their only hope—Puck. But it wasn't Puck. Instead, it was the strange fairy they'd encountered in the woods. He slammed his feet into the dragon's snout, and the impact forced the beast's chin into the pavement, stunning it for a few moments. "You might want to leave this one to the expert."

The creature reared back and belched a ball of flame at the fairy, but he was too quick, darting back and forth with amazing speed and agility. The dragon was not discouraged. It let loose a dozen more blasts, getting closer to its target with each attempt. At least the fairy was successfully luring the monster away from Sabrina and Daphne.

"You have to come with us," said a voice from behind them. The girls spun around to find the blond warrior woman. She had her sword drawn, while her friend, the dark-haired woman, held a wand that glowed green with energy.

"We're not going anywhere with you," Sabrina said, stepping in front of her sister. She clenched her fists and scowled, preparing for a fight if the women wanted one. She set her feet the way Ms. White had taught her.

"There's no time to explain," the fair-haired woman said. "We have to get to safety. If they find you out here, they will kill you."

"Who?" Daphne cried. "Who will kill us?"

"The Scarlet Hand."

Before Sabrina could ask another question, the fairy snatched her and Daphne off the ground and hoisted them onto his shoulders like they were a couple of sacks of potatoes. The dark-haired woman reached into one of her many pockets and took out what appeared to be a tiny blue marble.

"Let us go!" Daphne demanded, but she was ignored. Instead, the woman with the marble tossed it at the fairy's feet and energy swirled around their bodies. It seemed to rush through Sabrina's body and dance on the edges of her mind. She looked over at her sister to find that Daphne's hair was standing on end. There was a bright flash of light, like someone snapping a picture, and then Sabrina felt an even more peculiar sensation. It wasn't painful, but it felt as if her body were being folded neatly into halves, then folded again, and again, and again, until she was a tiny fragment of herself—so small she was invisible. Then she was folded one last time, and everything went black.

When the lights came on, Sabrina found herself lying on a pile of rags in a filthy bedroom. Scattered about were musty books, old furniture, and boxes of strange trinkets. She scanned the room, puzzled by its familiarity. She looked up at the tarnished chandelier and then at a table covered in potions and books. One of them was bound with what looked like human skin. She fought a wave of revulsion as she realized where she was.

"We're inside Baba Yaga's house," Sabrina croaked.

"What?" Daphne said groggily. The little girl was lying right next to Sabrina. "I was having a dream about ice cream."

"Do you know how we got here?" Sabrina asked.

Daphne shook her head.

"It's really freaky," a voice said from behind them. Sabrina spun around to find the grown-up fairy sitting in a chair, watching over them. "When is your birthday?"

"Why do you want to know?"

"It has to be you. You're just as stubborn. C'mon, kid, just tell me when your birthday is."

"It's in two days," Sabrina replied suspiciously. "I'll be twelve."

The fairy sat up and stared closely at the girls. "Just when I thought I'd seen everything."

Just then, the warrior women entered the room.

"Well, it's them. Or it's you, I guess. This is confusing," the fairy said.

"I don't remember this happening," the dark-haired woman said. "But then again, we were always running off on our own back then."

The blond woman shook her head. "This definitely did not happen."

"What are you talking about?" Sabrina demanded.

"We should take them to the general," the dark-haired woman said, ignoring Sabrina's question.

"We should take them as far away from here as possible," the other woman argued. "Who knows what could happen if they got hurt."

"You should take us home," Sabrina interrupted. "Everything has gone crazy. The town is in ruins, there are dragons flying around, and Mr. Canis has lost control of the Wolf. I know he looks like a monster, but that thing you were fighting is our friend."

"That beast is no one's friend," the blond woman said sternly. "We barely escaped with our lives."

"You don't understand," Sabrina argued. "My family can help. We fix problems like this all the time. You need to let us go home."

"I'm afraid we can't do that," the fairy said.

"Oh yeah?" Sabrina challenged. "Who do you think you are, kidnapping us?"

The blond woman got onto one knee and extended a hand. "My name is Sabrina Grimm. This is my sister, Daphne Grimm, and my husband, Puck."

Sabrina and Daphne stared at them.

"You people are nutballs!" Sabrina cried.

"Mucho nutballs-o!"

The woman claiming to be Daphne ignored the insult. "House, head for the mountains!" she shouted, and suddenly, everyone was jostled around the room. If there had been any lingering doubt in Sabrina's mind that they were in Baba Yaga's home, it was now gone. Sabrina couldn't be sure, but she felt as if the house might be running at a full sprint.

The woman who claimed to be Sabrina helped the sisters to their feet. "I'm guessing you're pretty confused. I wish I could help explain what has happened, but we're just as bewildered. We'll sort this out as soon as we get back to camp."

"What camp?"

"The rebel camp," the fairy said.

The camp was really a fortress surrounded by high walls made of thick timber. It was built in the shape of a square. At each corner stood a tall lookout tower, equipped with a large cannonlike weapon. Sabrina watched from a window of Baba Yaga's house as an immense gate swung open to allow them to enter the compound. Once the witch's house was inside, the gate was closed again and then reinforced with beams to prevent it from being forced open from the outside.

Inside were a dozen tiny cabins made from stones, a small farm, and what looked like an elaborate obstacle course. Men and women rushed through it while a small man barked orders at them.

The house trotted over to a well and dropped awkwardly to the ground. Sabrina noticed long tubes running into the well from the lookout cannons, and she immediately understood that the weapons shot water, probably at dragons.

A moment later, the fairy who claimed to be Puck opened the door. Waiting outside was an elderly man wearing a burlap sack he had fashioned into a shirt and pants.

"How goes it, Faithful John?" the fairy asked, taking the man's hand and shaking it vigorously.

"All is quiet, so all is good," the man said with a smile.

"Where's the general?" the woman with the scar asked as she stepped outside.

"In the tent," Faithful John replied as he pointed to a large tent at the other end of the fortress.

Just then, there was a loud trumpeting. "Oh, William must have returned."

The doors of the fortress swung open once more as a great white horse charged through. A rugged man, dressed in torn purple slacks and a shirt that had once been white, sat astride. His hair was long and dark, and he held a sword in one hand and the horse's reins in the other. Sabrina and Daphne had to leap out of the horse's path for fear of being trampled.

"The Hand has a platoon of card soldiers by the river!" the man shouted. "Tell the general that we can attack at dusk."

Faithful John nodded and raced off.

As for the man on the horse, he dismounted while the entrance to the camp was once again secured. Sabrina took a closer look at him. He was shockingly handsome, despite his unkempt beard, long hair, and filthy clothing. There was also something very familiar about him, though she couldn't be sure what.

The man sensed her curiosity and turned to face her. Then, without warning, he wrapped the girls up in his arms and cried with happiness.

"How did you get here?"

Sabrina pulled herself away. "Uh, hello, personal space!"

"It's me. Prince Charming!"

"Nuh-uh," Daphne said, but Sabrina wasn't so sure. She studied his face, using her imagination to cut his hair and shave his beard. It didn't make sense, but it was clear that the man was telling the truth.

"It's him!" she exclaimed.

"Where did you come from?" he asked.

"We were out in the woods with Mr. Canis and—"

"Canis! Is he here, too?" the prince asked hopefully. Sabrina was confused. She had never heard Charming speak of their family friend with anything but disdain.

"He's out in the woods somewhere, and he's lost control to the Wolf. You have to help us," Sabrina said, struggling to believe that she was asking the notoriously grouchy prince for assistance. "These freaks kidnapped us before I could warn Granny and Uncle Jake."

"Yeah, the town has gone mucho crazy-o!" Daphne said.

"No. No, no, no! You don't have to worry about Mr. Canis. Everyone's better off where they are," Charming said as he ran his hand through his dusty hair. "In the past."

"Not you, too!" Sabrina groaned. "I've had it with this practical joke. What do you want me to say? I believe you? You've fooled me? Well, forget it. It takes a lot to pull a prank on me."

"It's not a prank," the blond warrior said. "Ferryport Landing has been like this for almost fifteen years."

"That's impossible!" Sabrina exclaimed as she felt Daphne slip her hand into her own and squeeze tightly.

"Sabrina," the woman continued, "I'm you. I'm twenty-six years old. In two days I'll be twenty-seven." She turned to the dark-haired woman she called her sister. "And this is Daphne."

Sabrina studied their faces. She had to admit the dark-haired woman did look like Daphne, but without all the light and happiness of her sister's face.

"And I'm Puck," the fairy said. His wings popped out of his back and lifted him several feet off the ground. He put his hands on his hips and grinned broadly. "Taa-daa!"

"Now I know this is a joke," Sabrina said, spinning on the fairy. "Everafters don't grow old."

"Not true, Sabrina. An Everafter can grow old if he wants. Most don't because they don't have a good reason," Puck said, sharing an affectionate look with the woman claiming to be Sabrina. The fairy had a gold ring on his left hand that was identical to one the older Sabrina wore.

Daphne squealed. "You mean . . . you and Puck . . . really . . . married!"

The older Sabrina grinned bashfully, then looked at the fairy. "He gets a little less annoying as he gets older."

"But only a little," the fairy said with a laugh. "We should introduce our guests to the general."

They walked to the tent Faithful John had pointed out to them. Charming pulled back the flaps and ushered the girls inside. The older versions of themselves and Puck followed. There they found a queen-size bed. Two adults lay on top of it, sound asleep.

"Mom! Dad!" the girls cried, and rushed to their side. Their parents' hair was gray, and wrinkles had formed in the corners of their eyes.

"They're still asleep," a voice said from behind them. It was old and crackling, but familiar. Sabrina turned around and saw an old woman in a wheelchair in the door of the tent.

"Girls, this is the general," Charming said.

The old woman wore a bright yellow dress and a matching hat with a sunflower appliqué at its center. Trotting around her chair were four Great Dane puppies.

"Granny Relda!" Daphne cried as she raced across the room and wrapped the old woman in a hug. Sabrina followed more slowly, shocked at how old Granny looked.

"There's a name I haven't heard in many years," the old woman said. She studied the girls' faces and then turned to their older counterparts with a confused expression.

"I'm blaming the weird weather, old lady," Puck said.

The group shared a meal of potatoes, venison, and black bread while the day's events were explained to the future version of Granny Relda. During the meal, she studied maps and reports shown to her by people who came and went, each following her orders. Sometime during the meal, a little man wearing a crude military uniform emblazoned with dozens of bright badges and medals entered the tent. He was the same man Sabrina had spotted training soldiers, but she recognized him immediately now that she saw him close up. He was Mr. Seven. He saluted the old woman with great respect, and they briefly discussed the forces at the riverside and agreed on the best strategy for attack. When the conversation was over, he saluted her again, then disappeared without glancing at the girls once.

"Don't be offended that he didn't speak to you," Granny Relda said. "Captain Seven is very busy."

"Captain?" Daphne asked.

"He's responsible for many of our army's successes," Charming explained.

"Why do you need an army?" Sabrina asked.

"To fight the Scarlet Hand, of course," Granny said as she tossed chunks of her dinner to her four impatient puppies. "Since the Master rose, we've been one of the main fronts in the battle for human freedom. There are other units scattered around the world, and I've been leading the charge. That's how I got my little nickname. The truth is, without Seven and the other brave members of our rebellion we wouldn't stand a chance. The Master and his Hand are relentless."

"So, it happened. The Scarlet Hand took over the world?" Daphne asked.

"They couldn't have done it if they hadn't plundered the Hall of Wonders," the grown-up Sabrina explained. "They got into the house, then into the mirror, and they opened every door. They took everything of value and set the monsters free. There were horrible things behind some of those doors. It threw the town into chaos."

She shared a knowing look with the old woman.

"One of those monsters tried to barbecue us today," Puck added.

"But how? Why didn't we stop it from happening?" Sabrina wondered.

"What can an old woman and two little girls do?" Granny Relda said, before breaking into a coughing fit. When she recovered, she continued.

"You're forgetting Elvis," Daphne said.

"He was a brave soul. These four pups are his great-grandchildren. Let me introduce you to John, Paul, George, and Ringo."

The dogs raced over to Daphne and sat with begging eyes until the girl surrendered her venison steak.

"Yep, they're related," Daphne said as she hugged them all.

"What about Uncle Jake?"

The old woman shifted uncomfortably in her chair.

"He was arrested and put into the Ferryport Landing jail," she said sadly. "They gave him a trial and sentenced him to life in prison, but he escaped. When they caught him, they killed him in our yard."

"I saw that happen!" Sabrina cried. "He was shot with an arrow."

"I don't remember that happening," the older Sabrina said.

"How can these things have occurred in the past but we don't remember them?" Puck asked. "Our Prince Charming didn't disappear. Uncle Jake wasn't murdered when the girls were young."

"We didn't just pop up in the future, either," the older Daphne said.

"How long have you been here?" Charming asked the girls.

"A couple of hours," Sabrina said.

"I've been trapped here for a couple of months," he said.

"So, you're not a future version of Prince Charming?" Sabrina asked, doing her best to understand all the new information.

"No, I'm from the past—I mean, the present . . . it's all very confusing. After the election I wanted to get away and clear my head. I was taking one last walk on the grounds of the mansion when a storm appeared out of nowhere. It took several hours for me to figure out that I wasn't where I was supposed to be. Now it's happened to you, too."

"So we're stuck here?" Sabrina asked.

Charming shrugged. "I don't know. All I know is that nothing I've tried has sent me back. Tell me, is Snow all right?"

Daphne nodded. "I mean, she's worried, but she's all right. She's been looking for you everywhere."

"I guess they'll be looking for us next," Sabrina said. A bubble of panic crawled up her throat. What if they were stuck in this dark future? What if they couldn't get back home? "What's causing this?"

The older Daphne cleared her throat. "I believe that time is tearing."

"Huh?" Daphne asked.

"Let me try to explain this the best I can. Imagine that time is like a tablecloth. Now imagine that something is stabbing holes into its fabric. When that happens the things on top of the tablecloth can fall through the holes. In this case, you and your sister and William fell through. Then imagine that there is some force in the universe that closes the hole, trapping everything that's fallen through on the other side."

"That's fascinating," Granny Relda said. "So the hole opens up and takes things from when Sabrina and Daphne were young and brings them here."

"It's just a theory," the older Daphne said. "I have very little experience with time travel. That's usually the realm of science, not magic."

"Only, the hole doesn't just connect our time with this one," Sabrina pointed out. "We saw a band of Native Americans from colonial times attack Baba Yaga this afternoon. I mean, our this afternoon."

"And we heard Nottingham complaining that there was some

man on Mount Taurus claiming to have seen dinosaurs," Daphne added.

"This sounds very dangerous," Granny Relda said.

"It could be. Every time one of those storms appears, a hole opens. Who knows what could walk through the next one," Puck said.

"I wonder if Baba Yaga remembers the attack?" Sabrina said.

"I'm afraid there's no way to ask her. The witch was one of the first of the resistance fighters to die," Granny Relda said. "She made a foolish error when she destroyed her guardians. She never replaced them, and it left her vulnerable. The Scarlet Hand cornered her in the forest and killed her, but not before she took out nearly forty of them."

"The house ran off," Puck said. "We found it cowering in the woods, and we've been using it ever since."

"Wait! Maybe all this has something to do with the case we're working on," Sabrina said.

"What case?" Granny Relda asked.

"Do you remember all those missing magic items that were stolen—Merlin's wand, the Wonder Clock, and the water from the Fountain of Youth? We're in the middle of a magical crime spree," Daphne said.

"I remember now," Granny Relda said. "We never solved that case."

"Unbelievable! The Relda Grimm I know would never let a mystery go unsolved," Charming said with a hint of disdain.

"There were other things, urgent things that needed our attention," the old woman said.

"The taxes?" Sabrina asked.

Granny Relda nodded in agreement. "Things just got worse and worse, and we never had time to do any more investigating."

"What got worse?" Sabrina asked suspiciously.

The adults were silent for a long, heartbreaking moment, trading distraught expressions.

"Show them the house," the older Daphne said.

"Don't you think that's a little harsh?" Puck asked.

"If we don't show them the truth, they will go and discover it for themselves. You remember how we used to be. We were always running off in the middle of the night," the grown-up Sabrina said. "Let them see it while we can protect them. Besides, if they get killed, we would die, too, right? They're us."

Granny Relda shrugged. "I guess it's for the best."

Sabrina and Daphne traded a worried look as the older versions of themselves led them all back to Baba Yaga's house.

As the house left the fortress, Sabrina watched out the window as they passed abandoned homes and a forest charred with black smoke. Roads were buckled and littered with abandoned cars.

After a while, the creepy shack came to a lumbering stop.

"We're here," the future Daphne said as she glanced through the window. "We can't stay long. The dragons circle the area in fifteen-minute cycles, and we don't know when the last one started."

Sabrina felt the house lower. Puck came from the other room with his crossbow and arrows in hand. He kicked open the door, took a peek outside, then gestured for everyone to follow. Sabrina and Daphne shuffled after him with Charming close behind.

And then they saw it, the plot of land that had once been their grandmother's home. Their house was gone, along with any sign that it had ever existed. Not even the trees were left behind. Instead, an enormous castle made from black stones sat in its place. Two high towers watched the land, and a moat snaked around the building. On top of one of the towers, a black flag fluttered in the wind. In its center was a bloodred handprint.

Sabrina could feel tears run down her face, and for the first time in her life she didn't try to hide them.

"I haven't been here in years," the older Sabrina said. "Never thought I'd be strong enough to look at it—"

"How do we fix this?" Sabrina interrupted.

"Fix it?" her older self said. "I don't know if you can fix it."

"We can stop this," Daphne said, her own face wet with tears. "Now that we know what is going to happen, we can make sure it doesn't."

Charming nodded. "My plan exactly, if I can ever get back."

"People, get back into the house! NOW!" Puck shouted as he pointed his crossbow toward the sky.

Sabrina looked up and gasped. A dragon sailed overhead. It was green, black, and red, with puffs of smoke drifting out of its wide snout. Its roar shook the earth, and from its gruesome jaws came a blast of flame that turned a nearby stump into black ash.

The older Sabrina helped Granny wheel her chair into Baba Yaga's house. The rest of the group followed and slammed the door behind them.

"House! Let's move it!" the older Sabrina shouted, and the building once again rose to its feet and raced into the woods.

"Can we outrun that?" Sabrina asked as she watched the dragon roast another nearby tree.

"No," the older Daphne said, rushing to the window and nudging the girls aside. She threw it open and pointed a long, thin wand outside. Water blasted out of the wand as if it were a firefighter's hose. Unfortunately, her aim was off and the stream hit the beast in the chest instead. She cursed herself and shook the wand angrily.

"Not feeling well today, marshmallow?" Puck said. "'Cause if so, I could go out and fight it myself."

"I'm tempted to let you," she replied. "And don't call me that ridiculous nickname."

Daphne stuck her tongue out at her older self. "Hey, cranky, I like my nickname!"

Future Daphne fired her wand again, and another torrent of water exploded into the sky like a geyser. This time it hit the dragon squarely in the mouth. The beast tried to roar, but only a breathy squeak came out. The loss of its most deadly weapon seemed to hinder the dragon's ability to fly as well. It fell to the ground hard, disappearing from view.

"Nice shot, me," Daphne said.

"Unfortunately, it's only down temporarily," Granny Relda said. "Let's hope that we can put some distance between us and it before it reignites its pilot light."

Sabrina and Daphne slept on skinny cots. Sabrina was used to sharing a bed with her sister, and having her own felt strangely lonely. She was sure Daphne was just as troubled and wanted to talk, but when she called out to her she was met with a low, rumbling snore. Apparently the shock of their current situation wasn't causing Daphne any loss of sleep.

"Child," Charming called softly from his cot across the room.

Sabrina sat up and rubbed her eyes. "I'm awake."

"It's not so easy to sleep knowing what we know, is it?"

"I'm having trouble keeping it all straight," she admitted. "I do need to know one thing. How did Daphne get hurt? I mean, the older Daphne. How did she get that scar?"

"It was my fault. I asked her to help me find something. It was dangerous, and we ran into trouble," Charming said.

"What kind of trouble?"

"Nottingham."

Sabrina shuddered, imagining the wicked sheriff's dagger.

"I needed to recover something," Charming said. "Something that might help us go home. But Nottingham is guarding it, and he . . . well . . ."

Just then, the older Daphne entered the tent. "Another storm has been spotted," she said to Charming.

"You think it's a time hole?"

"I do," she said. "It's at the Ferryport Landing Cemetery. We need to leave now."

Together, the group crept through rows of headstones as far as the eye could see. Weeds grew over most of the burial plots. None of the cemetery's lamps were working, so the group relied on the bluish light of the full moon. It gave everything a ghostly quality.

"I can't guarantee the storm will take you back to your time," the older Daphne said. "In fact, it could put you into an even more dangerous situation."

"What could be more dangerous than running from dragons all day long?" Sabrina asked.

"Appearing in the past during the witch trials, for one." her older self replied. "Imagine popping up in a Puritan camp and being burned at the stake. Or you could be sent further into the future, when my sister and I are dead and there is no one to protect you from the Scarlet Hand."

"So, we could step through the tear only to find a hungry Tyrannosaurus rex on the other side?" Sabrina asked.

"No, T-rexes weren't native to North America," her older self explained matter-of-factly. "But you could step through and find yourself in an ice age thousands of years in the past, or far into the future on the day the sun goes supernova. This isn't a ticket on the Metro-North train. We don't know when you'll end up."

"Then it's too dangerous," Granny Relda said.

"Relda, we can't stay here," Charming said. "If there's a chance to get back and make things right, we have to take it. I can't speak for the girls, but I'm going through."

"We'll take our chances, too," Daphne said.

Sabrina looked to her sister, surprised by her boldness but nodding in agreement. A little chance was better than no chance at all.

Future Daphne gazed up at the menacing sky swirling above their heads. "Here it comes. Are you ready?"

Everyone nodded.

"So how do we know where the tear opens?" Charming asked impatiently.

The future Daphne took a small black orb out of one of her pockets. It shimmered like water. "My magic detector is pointing to that grave," she said, gesturing toward a headstone covered in weeds.

Charming's face blanched. He walked to the spot reluctantly, as if it pained him to stand near it. Sabrina and Daphne joined him and saw the name chiseled into the granite: SNOW WHITE.

Daphne gasped.

"They killed her," Charming said.

"Why?"

Charming shook his head miserably. He knelt down and caressed the granite as if it were Snow's delicate face. "I will change this," he promised. Then he stood, grabbing Sabrina and Daphne by the arms.

"We'll help you. We have to change everything we can," Daphne said.

Just then, the black cloud churned like an angry whirlpool. The abrupt change in the sky was startling.

"That's it!" the older Daphne shouted. The black orb was pulsating with light. It was even causing its owner to vibrate. "It's coming."

"Take care of yourselves, girls," the older Granny Relda said as the cloud got wider and uglier.

"And take care of each other!" the grown-up Sabrina said.

"You, too!" Daphne shouted over the wind roaring in their ears.

"Am I interrupting another tender moment?" a voice asked

with a loud growl. The group turned to find the Wolf approaching. "I hope you don't mind. I brought some friends."

Behind him, Sabrina spotted what appeared to be a small army. They raced toward the group, holding spears, swords, and bows and arrows. On each of their chests was a bloodred handprint. It was the army of the Scarlet Hand.

The future Daphne reached into her overcoat and took out a wand. She turned it on the Wolf and a powerful shockwave hit the beast, sending him flailing backward over the high trees. Unfortunately, it did not slow the approaching soldiers.

"I'm on it," the older Sabrina said.

"Sister . . ." the future Daphne started, but the blond woman was already leaping into action.

Puck swooped down, scooped the future Sabrina up, and flew her straight toward the approaching soldiers. The two disappeared into the throng, and moments later Sabrina could hear the sounds of clanging swords, groaning men, and Puck's cheers and laughter.

Sabrina heard something zip through the air and saw an arrow land only inches away from her foot. Another arrow whizzed past and hit a nearby tree. She pulled her sister close. "I hope this thing is going to happen soon."

The future Daphne raced to Charming's side and pointed to her face. "Make sure Nottingham pays for this."

Sabrina looked at the jagged scar on the woman's cheek. She hoped the rough winds had prevented young Daphne from hearing the terrible conversation.

"I will!" Charming shouted.

Sabrina had a million questions, but she never got a chance to ask them. At that moment the world dissolved right before her eyes.

7

SABRINA WOKE TO FIND HERSELF LYING IN THE suddenly well-manicured Ferryport Landing Cemetery. The moon was bright in the sky, and her sister and Charming were lying next to her. The smell of fire and brimstone was gone. She held her breath and waited for the approaching army to break the silence, but after a few moments, all she could hear were crickets chirping in the grass. She sat up and smiled. She couldn't be sure they were home, but it felt right.

Charming rubbed his eyes. He looked up at the sky then turned and looked behind him. Snow White's gravestone was gone. In fact, the trio was lying in a completely unused portion of the cemetery.

"Do you think we're back?" Daphne asked.

"It appears so," Charming replied. "Though I don't know what day it is."

Sabrina scanned the horizon. She spotted a thin trail of smoke rising into the clouds. "Well, let's go ask someone," she said as she scrambled to her feet. She helped Daphne and Charming up, and they marched in the direction of the smoke. They walked until they found a log cabin. Sabrina's heart froze. Had they returned to the days of the American frontier?

"We're back where we're supposed to be," Charming said as he pointed out the fancy sports car parked in the driveway. "That's the latest model. I had my eye on one before I lost my job."

Charming pounded on the cabin's door, demanding a ride to town, but he only managed to terrorize the homeowner, who swore he'd call the police if the filthy man and his "ragamuffin children" didn't get off his property. Sabrina was so angry she could have kicked the prince. If he'd just knocked like a normal person and asked nicely, the three of them might have already been on their way back to the house. Apparently three months in a doomsday future hadn't stripped Charming of his sense of entitlement.

"Then at least tell me what day it is," Charming demanded.

"I'm calling the cops right now, you lunatic!" the man shouted back.

So they were forced to walk. Sabrina's feet were already sore from her previous trek into town. Charming spent much of the trip attempting to make his tattered clothing and ratty hair look presentable.

Several hours later, the trio arrived at Granny Relda's. The house was a very welcome sight, but Charming stopped the girls before they could enter.

"We should get our story straight," he said.

Sabrina was stunned. "What story? We went into the future. We need their help to change everything that's going to happen."

"Child, are you really going to go in there and tell everyone you love that they are going to have tragic futures? Your uncle murdered, Canis a savage beast?"

"It is kind of a downer," Daphne said. "But what choice do we have?"

"You have the choice to say nothing," Charming said. "Listen, you have to trust me on this, because I've had a lot longer to think about what I'd do when I got back than the two of you. I know exactly how Snow dies. I know who kills her—but if I tell her, and word gets out about it, the killer could change his plans. I wouldn't know when it was going to happen, and I wouldn't be able to stop it. Telling everyone what you know will not help change things. Do you understand? It's best if we keep this to ourselves. We can work in the shadows. We can fix things without anyone knowing or interfering."

Sabrina looked into Charming's eyes. She could tell he truly believed what he was saying. Sharing what they had seen could lead to bigger, unexpected problems. Still, could she trust him? Charming could be selfish and underhanded, and it was no secret that he disliked her family. But, she had to admit, he'd always been honest.

"You want us to work together?" Sabrina asked.

"What choice do we have? I'm not thrilled about it, either, but together we can fix everything, including waking up your parents. I have resources that can help make that happen. I can also help find those stolen items and solve the case. We have to fix everything, girls. Everything! But we can't let anyone get in our way, even if they mean well, even if we love them." Charming paused. "Or, we could do it your way and just spill the beans. Let's go in the house and tell that fairy boy of yours that you are married to him in the future."

Sabrina stopped in her tracks and narrowed her eyes at the former mayor. "You wouldn't."

"If we tell, we tell everything," he said.

She could already feel her face turning red with embarrassment.

Charming laughed. "How does that song go? Sabrina and Puck, sitting in a tree, K-I-S-S-I-N-G. First comes love—"

Sabrina watched as her sister started to join the song.

"Shut your traps!" she shouted at both of them. "Fine! We'll do it your way—for now."

Charming nodded. "Very good! Finally, a Grimm who is reasonable!"

The door flew open, and Granny and Uncle Jake rushed outside. They ran across the lawn and wrapped Sabrina and Daphne in bearlike hugs. Elvis followed, knocking Daphne to the ground and covering her in sloppy kisses.

"*Lieblings!* Oh, thank goodness!" their grandmother cried. "We've been looking for you for hours."

The happy reunion didn't last long. Mr. Canis raced across the lawn and snatched Charming off the ground with one of his clawed hands. "If you have touched a hair on their heads, so help me . . ."

"Mr. Canis, put him down! He didn't hurt us!" Sabrina insisted.

Canis ignored Sabrina's plea. "What happened to the two of you?"

"We got lost," Sabrina said. She gave her sister a quick look to make sure she was okay with the lie. Daphne nodded.

Canis scowled. "I would have found you if you were lost."

"Well, you blew it," Charming replied as he fought to free himself. "I found the two ragamuffins wandering in the woods, and I helped them get here. Now, put me down, you filthy mongrel."

Canis turned to Granny Relda. The old woman nodded, and he set the prince back down on his feet.

"And where have you been?" Granny asked Charming. "You've been missing for two months. My family has torn this town apart looking for you. Snow is out of her mind with worry. You should call her right away."

Charming shook his head. "I would appreciate if you kept my reappearance a secret for now. I'll explain what I've been doing when the time is right, but for now, I must be going."

"Where?" Daphne said. "You're sort of homeless."

"She's right, pal," Uncle Jake added. "When you lost the election you lost your mansion. The Queen of Hearts lives there now."

"Oh," Charming said as he stared off at the horizon. "I suppose you're right."

Sabrina couldn't believe what came out of her own mouth next. "You can stay with us."

Granny gasped, then forced a smile. She put her hand on Sabrina's forehead. "Are you feeling well?"

"I'm feeling fine, Granny," Sabrina said. If the girls were going to help Charming change the future, it was probably best if he was close by. Sure, he was an arrogant jerk, especially when it came to the Grimms, but she could tolerate a barrage of insults if it would help avert disaster. "I think Mr. Charming needs some time to get on his feet. He'd do the same for us."

"Don't bet on it," Uncle Jake said.

"Uh . . . Sabrina is right," Granny stammered. "We . . . uh . . . don't have a lot of room, Billy, but you're welcome to stay. The sofa is very comfortable."

"What?" Canis growled.

"I couldn't," Charming said.

"He's right," Mr. Canis said. "He couldn't."

"Billy, we insist," Granny said.

"You can't be serious," Canis argued. "He can't be trusted. Don't you recall that he has threatened to destroy this family?"

"I may be old, but my memory is still intact," the old woman said defensively. "Everyone deserves a second chance."

"This man will stab you in the back the first chance he gets. Don't be such a fool!" Canis snapped.

"There was a time when people said the same thing about you," Relda said angrily. After a moment she took a deep breath. "Mr. Canis, the decision has been made."

She took Charming by the arm and led him into the house.

Canis flashed a look at Sabrina that was both bewildered and betrayed. Sabrina blushed, realizing she had just invited the old man's bitterest enemy to live with them. Canis looked angrier than she had ever seen him—and worse, his anger was directed at her grandmother. Sabrina had never seen Granny Relda and Mr. Canis bicker before. It made her nervous, especially now that she knew the destiny that lay ahead for the old man. Who knew what would make Canis snap and finally surrender to the Wolf?

"Nice suggestion, 'Brina," Uncle Jake said as they watched Canis stomp off into the trees. "You sure you didn't fall and hit your head out in those woods?"

Sabrina and Daphne followed Jake inside, where they found Charming eyeing the couch disdainfully. He turned toward the window and looked outside, as if weighing his options, then turned back and fluffed up one of the couch cushions. "You are all very kind. I'll try to stay out of the way."

Puck came down the steps and looked at the girls. "I heard you two were missing," he said to Sabrina.

"We're back," she replied.

"Darn," he grumbled, then turned and walked back up the steps.

"There goes your future husband," Daphne whispered in Sabrina's ear.

She knew her face was as red as a fire truck. How was she going to get used to being around Puck now that she knew she was destined to marry the smelly, rude boy?

Sabrina lay still in her father's old bed. Daphne tossed and turned next to her.

"I'm afraid to go to sleep," the little girl whispered.

"We're back," Sabrina responded. "That's what matters. We're back, and we can make a difference."

"What if we can't?" Daphne asked.

Sabrina flipped on the light and crossed the room to her father's old desk. She opened a drawer and pulled out a hairbrush. Daphne's eyes lit up when she saw it. Brushing Sabrina's hair always calmed Daphne.

"We will," Sabrina promised. "The first step is solving the case."

Suddenly, there was a soft tapping at their door. It creaked open and Charming popped his head inside.

"Get dressed and meet me downstairs," he hissed. "We've got work to do."

The girls did as they were told. They found Charming waiting by the front door. He was wearing a pair of Uncle Jake's jeans, a white sweater, and one of their late grandfather's coats.

"What's the plan, Stan?" Daphne asked.

Charming gestured for her to be silent and then ushered them outside into the cool night. He closed the door tightly, and Sabrina told the house they would be back soon, activating the magical lock.

"I have a few items I need to retrieve, and I could use the extra hands," Charming said.

"Items? What kind of items?"

"The kind that change the future for the better," he said. "Unfortunately, they happen to be at the mansion."

Sabrina was shocked. "The mansion! We can't go there. Mayor Heart lives there now. She's got guards!"

"Guards with swords!" Daphne added. "Sharp, pointy swords."

"Yes, I suppose she does," the prince said as if that were a small, irrelevant detail.

"Besides, what makes you think she still has your things?" Sabrina asked. "From what I hear, she's broken the bank redecorating the mansion. Anything you left behind is probably at the town dump by now."

"Not these things," he said. "If I know Heart like I think I do, she would never throw these out. Oh look, here comes our ride."

Just then, two bright headlights blinded Sabrina as a car pulled into the driveway. When her eyes adjusted, she realized she was looking at a long white limousine. The driver's side door opened and a dwarf in a black tuxedo stepped out.

"Good evening, Seven," Charming said.

The dwarf nodded curtly. "Good evening."

"Thank you for taking my call," Charming said, looking down at the ground and shuffling his feet uncomfortably. In the future, Charming seemed to have tremendous respect for Mr. Seven. But in the present, the little man was Charming's former assistant, and the ex-mayor hadn't been a very nice boss. Seven had been subjected to a steady onslaught of insults and humiliations. Despite it all, the dwarf had stayed incredibly loyal to the prince. Of course, that was when Charming could pay him. Now, the former mayor had nothing to offer the little man.

Charming shuffled back and forth as if wrestling with a long overdue apology. Finally, all he could muster was a pat on Seven's back and a mumbled "Sorry."

"That is greatly appreciated, sir," Seven said as he rushed to open the door for Charming and the girls. "Your chariot awaits."

Moments later they were pulling away from the house and zipping through the back roads of Ferryport Landing.

"So tell us, what's so important that we have to risk life and limb to sneak into the mansion?" Sabrina asked.

"Among other things, a magic detector," Charming said.

"A what?" Daphne asked.

"A device that senses magic," Charming repeated. "Your older self used it to track the time tears. She and I tracked it down during my time in the camp. I think giving it to you now should be our first act of changing the future."

Daphne smiled. "Thanks!"

"That's hardly going to fix things, is it?" Sabrina asked.

Charming nodded. "It could help fix some things. It will allow the two of you to find the stolen magical devices and solve the case. We just need to be very careful to avoid Nottingham."

"Turn the car around," Sabrina said to Mr. Seven. The little man raised his eyebrows in surprise.

"What are you saying?" Charming said.

"I know what happened when you and future Daphne went to

retrieve the magic detector," she replied, flashing her eyes toward Daphne. In her mind, she could still see the jagged scar that ran down the future Daphne's face. "I won't let that happen."

"Neither will I," Charming said, understanding her concern. "I made a promise . . ."

"What are the two of you talking about?" Daphne demanded.

"I won't let Daphne get hurt!" Sabrina cried.

"There's no reason to believe that what happened to her in the future has to happen now," Charming reassured Sabrina.

"Oh, I get it," Daphne said. "The scar on my face. Nottingham did it."

Sabrina stared out the window. Charming looked at his shoes.

"You don't have to be a genius to figure out that I get hurt in the future trying to find this magic detector," the little girl said. "But we have to do this. Solving the case might make a huge difference. I'd rather have a scar than let the world turn out the way it does, or did, or whatever."

"Daphne, I—"

"It's my choice," the little girl interrupted.

"Sabrina, putting this tool into your sister's hands will make a difference," Charming said, then turned his attention to his driver. "Mr. Seven, what do you know about security at the mansion?"

"Heart's got guards at all the doors and windows," Seven said. "Plus a few roaming around the house. She's a little on the paranoid side and is convinced someone is going to try to come in and kill her in the night. Nottingham has moved in to keep an eye on her."

"The mayor is smarter than she looks," Charming said. "Good work, Seven."

"Thank you, sir."

The limousine snaked its way through the town until it reached the base of the mayor's long driveway. Seven helped everyone out of the car, then opened the trunk. Charming scooped out a pile of rope and some flashlights.

"This could get dangerous," Charming said to his former assistant.

"Danger is my middle name," Mr. Seven replied.

"I thought your middle name was Albert," Charming said.

"It is, sir. I was making a joke."

"Oh," Charming said. "A joke? I see. I suppose this new relationship of ours is going to take some getting used to."

Seven nodded.

"If Charming gets a sense of humor," Sabrina whispered to her sister, "that would totally change the future."

"Listen, Seven, are you sure you want to help?"

"I'm in, boss," the little man said as he got back into the limo.

Seven drove down the driveway toward the house while Charming led the girls onto the property on foot. They darted from tree to tree as they got closer and closer to the mansion. It wasn't long before they spotted some of the mayor's guards: men with arms, heads, and legs like people but torsos that were extra-large playing cards.

"What is Mr. Seven going to do?" Daphne asked.

"He's going to cause a distraction," Charming explained. "It will give us a shot at getting into the house undetected."

They tiptoed in the shadows, passing a fountain that had once featured a statue of Charming at its center. Now it contained a marble sculpture of the Queen of Hearts, though it was substantially thinner and more attractive than the real person. Mr. Seven had parked the limo next to it, and when he opened the door, an obnoxious dance song blasted through the car's brutally loud speakers.

"He's going to get us caught," Sabrina said.

"Just wait," Charming snapped, as if irritated that she would question the details of his plan.

"Here they come," Daphne said, pointing at half a dozen of the playing-card guards. They raced to the limo, shouted over the music, and leveled their swords at Mr. Seven's head. Sabrina couldn't make out their conversation, but they seemed to be arguing. A moment later, the front door flew open and Nottingham stormed out, dressed in a robe and slippers. His dagger was in his hand.

"What in the blazes is going on out here?" he bellowed.

"He says he's here to pick up Mayor Heart!" one of the guards responded. All the fuss kept the guards busy long enough for the trio to make their way around to the back of the house. Once there, Charming tried the handle on the back door, but it was locked.

"I should have known it wasn't going to be that easy," he said, pulling the rope off his shoulder. One end had a grappling hook attached to it. He tossed it onto the roof and it caught on something sturdy. He yanked it hard as a test and gestured to Sabrina.

"You want me to climb this?" Sabrina said.

"Looking at it is not going to get you onto the roof," Charming sneered.

Sabrina shrugged, grabbed onto the rope, and pulled with all her might. She'd learned to climb ropes in gym class. The trick wasn't in the shoulders or the arms, it was in the feet. Wrapping the rope around her heels kept her from sliding down and made the whole effort much easier. Soon she was on the roof, looking down at her sister and the prince. Charming let Daphne leap onto his back, and a few anxious moments later, they joined Sabrina.

Charming hurried to the chimney and peered down into it.

"Good—she hasn't built a fire."

Meanwhile, Sabrina was quickly pulling up the rope. Her heart nearly stopped when one of the guards rushed across the yard below her. He ran right by the rope, and though he didn't seem to see it in the darkness, it flicked against the back of his neck. He threw up his hand as if he were shooing a mosquito and kept moving. He would have certainly discovered the rope by his ear if Sabrina weren't pulling as quickly as she could.

"Bring it over here," Charming whispered.

The prince fastened the grappling hook to a rain gutter and gave it a good yank. The gutter creaked but held stable. Then he tossed the loose end of the rope down into the chimney and hoisted Daphne onto his back.

"We'll go first," he said. "If there happens to be someone waiting for us at the bottom, climb back down to the lawn and run to your grandmother."

"But you have the rope," Sabrina reminded him.

"Well, then, I guess we're all in deep trouble if there's someone down there."

He climbed into the chimney, and Sabrina watched them descend into the darkness below. After several moments, she decided it was her turn. She grabbed the rope tightly and lowered herself down.

In no time at all, her nose and mouth filled with soot. All the dust made breathing impossible. She leaned against the chimney wall with her back and used her feet to lock herself into place. Then she pulled her collar up over her nose and mouth, and took shallow breaths until the itching in her throat stopped and she could continue on.

Unfortunately, climbing down in the narrow space was extremely difficult. Sabrina kept knocking her knees and knuckles against the rough bricks of the chimney. She scraped her back so hard she cried out, and before she knew it she was hitting the floor with a thud. Luckily, she wasn't injured. She looked around to get her bearings and saw the opening of the fireplace before her. If she craned her neck, she could see into the mansion's grand hall. She was just about to crawl out to find Charming and Daphne when she saw two sets of unfamiliar feet.

"What does that moron want?" a woman asked. Sabrina recognized the grating voice. It was Mayor Heart.

"He says you hired a limousine to take you to a bachelorette party," the second voice said. Sabrina knew that one as well—it was Nottingham, and he was enraged.

"That's nonsense," Mayor Heart declared. "Send him away."

"I'm trying, but the little fool won't listen," Nottingham replied. "I suspect he may be dim in the head."

"Then can't you cut it off and be done with him? I need my rest."

Just then, there was a shuffle of feet and another man's voice said, "The driver has departed, Sheriff."

"Very good," Nottingham said. "Go back to your post."

"As you wish, sir."

When the man was gone, the wicked duo continued their conversation.

"Nottingham, I'm very distraught over all this. I doubt I will ever get to sleep now, unless . . ."

"Don't even think about it!" the sheriff said.

"But my bunions are killing me. Come to my room and rub my feet," Mayor Heart demanded.

"Absolutely not!"

"But it's the only thing that puts me to sleep!"

"Try counting tax payments. It eases me to sleep every night."

"DO IT OR I WILL HAVE YOUR HEAD CHOPPED OFF!"

There was a long pause.

"You get fifteen minutes," Nottingham replied. "Not a second more."

"Oh, you're an angel," Mayor Heart said sweetly.

Moments later they were gone, and Sabrina crawled out of the fireplace. She scanned the room for Charming and Daphne and spotted them hiding behind a gaudy curtain. They rushed to her side, with smirks on their faces. Daphne was pointing at Sabrina and trying to hide her laughter.

"What?" Sabrina whispered angrily.

"You seem to have gotten a little soot on you when you came down the chimney," Charming said.

Sabrina stepped over to a mirror hanging on the wall. In the moonlight she could see she was completely covered in black ash. Her hair, clothes—everything was filthy. Worse, she was starting to feel itchy. She gritted her teeth and turned back to the pair. Neither had a speck of dust on them.

"Naturally," she grumbled. "What now?"

"Follow me," Charming whispered. He led the girls through the rooms on the first floor. He opened each door and took a quick peek inside. Whatever he was looking for was not downstairs, so they continued his search on the second floor. It wasn't long before they exhausted their search there, too.

"It's in her room," Charming mumbled. "It has to be. We're going to have to go in there."

"What?" Daphne protested. "Nottingham is in there."

Charming ignored her. Before the girls could argue further, he opened a door and dragged them through.

Mayor Heart's room was a shrine to herself. There were pictures of her in various gaudy outfits, all of which were covered in little red hearts. Hanging over her bed was a huge ax that Sabrina was sure could easily lop a person's head clean off his shoulders. On the far wall leaned a full-length mirror. Nottingham was slumped in a chair by the mayor's bed. He was sound asleep with Heart's bunion-covered foot in his lap, mumbling something about taxes.

"This way," Charming whispered, tiptoeing toward the mirror.

"What are we looking for?" Sabrina grumbled as she watched the sleeping sheriff. In the moonlight from the window, she could see his dagger gleaming. A similar sparkle bounced off the ax. She imagined Heart and Nottingham springing from their beds and hacking the intruders to ribbons.

"Nottingham!" the mayor shouted, and bolted up in bed. She was wearing a sleeping mask and reached to remove it. Charming snatched the girls and threw them at the mirror's reflection. Sabrina cringed, expecting to smash the glass, but instead she and Daphne flew through it and landed on a marble floor. Charming followed them and turned back to look through the portal. They watched as Nottingham reluctantly got out of his chair and checked under the queen's bed and in her closets.

"We're in a magic mirror!" Daphne exclaimed.

Sabrina was too surprised to respond. She had been in their own mirror many times. The Hall of Wonders was a breathtaking place, but this magic mirror was entirely different. Instead of a long hallway lined with doors, this mirror looked like the lobby of a posh hotel. The floors were covered in beautiful Persian rugs. There were leather sofas and chairs scattered about. Spectacular chandeliers hung from the ceiling. A wall of windows revealed a beautiful sun-soaked beach just outside, complete with palm trees swaying in the breeze. Sabrina and Daphne approached the windows and gawked at the beautiful scenery. It had been a long time since the sun had shone so brightly in Ferryport Landing.

"Hello?" Charming called loudly. He stepped up to a long reception desk and leaned over it. "Hello?"

Just then, Sabrina heard a loud bell, and an elevator door opened behind them. A chubby Asian man wearing a Hawaiian shirt stepped out. His face was tanned and his eyes were lined with crow's feet. A big grin broke across his face.

"Boss! I knew you'd come back to rescue me. Where have you been?"

"I've been out of town, Harry," Charming said. "These are Relda Grimm's granddaughters."

"Aloha," he said as he clapped his hands. "Welcome to the Hotel of Wonders. I'm your host, Harry. Checking in?"

"I'm afraid not," Charming said. "I've just come to fetch a few things from my room."

"Of course, sir," Harry said. He rushed behind the reception desk and opened a drawer containing a collection of old-fashioned hotel keys.

"You own a magic mirror?" Sabrina asked.

"There is more than one, you know," Charming said.

"Mirror never told us that." Daphne said.

Harry led the group into the elevator and pushed a button that read PENTHOUSE. The elevator had glass walls, allowing the girls to gaze out on the beach and the blue ocean beyond as they ascended.

"Is this real?" Daphne asked.

"As real as you want it to be," Harry said, then turned to Charming. "Boss, you have to get me out of here. Every day, Heart gets dressed in front of me. A mirror can only take so much."

"Don't worry. You'll be leaving with us," Charming said.

"Thank heavens." Harry turned to the girls. "So, I heard you mention you have a mirror of your own?"

Sabrina nodded. "Yes, his name is Mirror."

"Ah yes, the prototype. Odd that he hasn't given himself a name yet," Harry remarked as the elevator stopped and the doors opened. He led the group down a hallway decorated with paint-ings. Every detail of the hotel was beautiful.

"I'm confused," Sabrina said. "How many magic mirrors are there?"

"Oh, that's hard to say! A lot, I suppose. The Wicked Queen invented your Mirror and then found she had a lot of customers wanting their own. Each mirror was intended to fill the particular needs of a client. I was one of the deluxe packages, designed to Mr. Charming's impeccable tastes, but there are also mirrors that look like desert islands, ski resorts, and even one that appears to be a Polish restaurant in Cleveland, Ohio.

"The prince needed a retreat, a place where he could get away and relax, so naturally the Hotel of Wonders was perfect for him," Harry said proudly. "It's a full-service luxury hotel fit for a prince."

Daphne looked up at Charming. "I always wondered how you stayed so tan."

"Oh, here we are." Harry said. He stopped at a door with a bronze plaque that read THE ROYAL SUITE. Harry unlocked the door, leading the group inside where they found a lavish suite complete with a king-size bed. There was an enormous Jacuzzi and a fireplace in the bathroom, and in an adjoining room was a lounge with an oak bar and big-screen television.

Harry opened two double doors, revealing a walk-in closet filled with expensive suits and shoes. Charming selected a long white jacket, which he laid on the bed. Then he picked out a clean black suit, some socks and shoes, and a tie. He laid these on the inside lining of the jacket, where they magically disappeared.

"Cool! What is that?" Daphne asked.

Charming nodded. "It's called the Hungry Jacket. It acts like a bag, storing things until I want them, when I can just reach in and take them out."

"It would come in real handy when we get the secret weapon," Daphne said.

Sabrina flashed the little girl an angry look.

"What secret weapon?" the former mayor asked.

Daphne whistled innocently.

"What secret weapon?" Charming pressed.

Sabrina knew they couldn't hide it any longer. "Show him."

Daphne took the necklace from around her neck and showed Charming the key. "Sheriff Hamstead gave this to us. He said it unlocked a safe-deposit box that holds a secret weapon we can use in case Mr. Canis loses control of the Wolf. We're not supposed to get it unless he does, and we're not supposed to tell anyone we have it."

Charming held the key in his hand for a moment, then gave it back to the girl. "Interesting," he murmured. "Whatever it is must be very powerful."

"What else would you like to take, boss?" Harry said. "The Cap of Knowledge has been cleaned as you requested. I'm sorry to say that the rust stains on the Sword of Sharpness are proving to be impossible to remove."

"I won't be needing either of them, Harry," Charming said. He laid some more clothes in the center of the jacket and Sabrina watched as they vanished. "But I will be needing the magic detector."

Harry rushed to a drawer across the room. From it, he pulled out a small black ball, no bigger than a marble and identical to the one Sabrina had seen future Daphne use. Charming took it from Harry and handed it to Daphne. The little girl marveled at it for a moment. "I feel funny," she said, "like I'm vibrating." Sabrina realized her sister was doing just that. It was disturbing for Sabrina to see the little girl shaking so hard. She wondered if it hurt.

"You're detecting magic," Charming said. "That should help you find the missing magic items."

"This town is filled with magic items," Sabrina said. "How do we narrow it down?"

"At first, Daphne will feel the things with the greatest power," Charming explained. "But if she concentrates it will lead her to specific objects. You're going to have to practice," he said to Daphne. "Now, let's go. I've got to get you home before you're missed."

"No time for a break, boss? The spa is offering hot-stone massages," Harry said as he closed the doors to the closet.

"Not today, Harry," Charming replied. "Though my neck could definitely use it. Perhaps next time."

"As you wish," Harry sang. He led them back to the elevator and through the lobby to the portal back to Mayor Heart's bedroom. Sabrina peered through it and saw the mayor sleeping soundly. Nottingham was nowhere in sight.

"I think the coast is clear," she told the others.

"It was a pleasure having you here in the hotel. Perhaps you two could come for a longer stay sometime," Harry said.

Charming flashed Harry a warning look.

"Or maybe not," Harry said. "Aloha and happy surfing."

Charming was the first to step through the portal. Sabrina and Daphne followed, and they were met with the sound of Heart's heavy snoring. Charming gestured for the girls to be still, then draped the white jacket over the mirror. When he pulled the garment away, the mirror was gone.

"Nice trick," Sabrina whispered.

With the jacket over his arm, Charming crossed the room and carefully opened the door. He peeked into the hallway and then gestured for the others to follow. Soon they were back at the fireplace.

"I'll go first," Sabrina said, reaching into the cramped space. "Something's wrong." She felt around frantically. "The rope is gone."

"Of course it's gone," a voice said from the darkness. "I can't just let people break in and out of the mayor's house whenever they want. I suggest you surrender now and avoid getting hurt."

Charming clamped his hands over the girls' mouths and pulled them close to him. He moved them quietly through the room, careful to stay away from any light that could reveal their identities, while also avoiding Nottingham's blade. It wasn't easy. The sheriff lunged forward, slashing the air wildly. The only good news was that he didn't appear to know who had invaded Heart's home, or where to find them in the dark.

"Whoever you are, you're either brave or stupid," Nottingham said. "Not many would break into the Mayor's house. You get points for cleverness, too. Crawling down the chimney was brilliant. I'll be sure to post a guard on the roof from now on."

Nottingham lunged again. This time, Charming threw a punch that caught the sheriff in the face. While he was recovering from the blow, Charming ushered the girls into another part of the room.

Nottingham roared with indignation. Sabrina guessed his pride hurt more than his face. He leaped at them, swinging his deadly blade in every direction. The girls and Charming stumbled backward to avoid the sheriff as best as they could. Unfortunately, the dagger snagged Charming's arm. There was a tearing sound, and the prince let out a groan.

"Aha!" Nottingham cried. He chased Charming around the room, knocking over tables and lamps. Glass crashed to the floor, furniture was overturned, and in the chaos, the sheriff caught his foot on an upturned rug. He fell forward, knocking Daphne to the ground. Without hesitation, Sabrina leaped on top of him, kicking and punching as hard as she could in hopes of freeing her little sister. Nottingham, however, was unfazed by Sabrina's attack and held his shiny dagger up to Daphne's face. She cried out, terrified.

"Why, you're just a child," Nottingham said. "Well, if you won't show me your face perhaps I will leave my mark on you, so I can recognize you in the light of day."

He raised the dagger high over his head, but before its tip could mar the little girl's face, Charming kicked Nottingham hard in the ribs. The blade flew out of his hand and skidded across the floor. The prince didn't give the sheriff a chance to recover. He punched

him square in the face. Sabrina heard a bone crack, and Nottingham bellowed in pain, then fell over a chair and hit his head on the floor. After that, he was silent and still.

"Add that to the list of things we changed about the future," Charming said, standing over the fallen villain.

8

MR. SEVEN DROPPED THE TRIO OFF OUTSIDE of Granny Relda's house. Charming thanked him for his help, but his thank-you was as stiff and awkward as his earlier apology. It was almost like watching a tree try to give someone a hug. When the little man was gone, the prince turned to the girls.

"It's best if the two of you get back to bed," he said. "We don't want anyone to know we've been—"

"Children, go inside," a voice said from behind them. Sabrina looked up to find Mr. Canis waiting on the porch.

Sabrina could see rage in the old man's face. "Mr. Canis, we were—"

"Children, go inside," Canis repeated. "The prince and I need to have a conversation."

The argument began before the girls even opened the door.

"You have no right to take them from this house," Canis said.

"It couldn't be helped. I got them back safely," Charming argued.

"Back from where exactly?"

"I can't tell you. You're just going to have to trust me," the prince said.

"Trust you?" Canis growled. "Only a fool would trust you!"

"Interesting coming from a man who is turning into a monster," Charming bellowed. "Listen, mutt, you want something to trust? Then trust this! I will always work in my own interests. Right now, it is in my interest to protect these girls. It is not because I care for them, or have deluded myself into believing that I am part of their family, like you! It's because their well-being serves my needs. They were perfectly safe."

"Take them from this home one more time without permission, and I will kill you," Canis said.

Charming marched up the porch stairs and into the house.

"Do you wish to explain?" Canis asked the girls, who were frozen on the porch.

Sabrina dipped her head, unable to look the old man in the eye. She couldn't bring herself to lie to him.

"I'm sorry. We can't tell you," Daphne said. "We made a promise."

"Get to bed," Canis snapped.

MAGIC AND OTHER MISDEMEANORS

The next morning, Sabrina woke to the loud thumping of people rushing up and down the stairs. She shook her sister awake. When they threw open their bedroom door, they found Uncle Jake and Mr. Canis moving furniture out of their grandmother's room.

"What's going on?" she said.

"We're having a yard sale," Granny said as she stepped out of her room. "Get dressed and come down right away. We need all the hands we can get."

The girls did as they were told and found a crowd of Everafters already gathered on the front lawn. They were browsing tables covered with lamps, old books, vases, and assorted knickknacks. All of the items had little red price tags on them. Granny sat at a rickety card table with a gray cash box in her lap.

"Why is she doing this?" Sabrina asked her uncle. He sat on the porch with his head in his hands.

"We're a little short on the new tax bill," he said.

"How short?"

"Three hundred thousand dollars short."

"Does she really think she's going to make that kind of money having a yard sale?" Sabrina asked.

"Desperate times call for desperate measures," Uncle Jake replied.

For most of the morning, people circulated through the tables, haggling over prices and chatting with neighbors. Granny stayed cheery throughout and never seemed insulted when she was told one of her prized possessions wasn't worth what she was asking for it. She rarely turned down an offer, even if it was ridiculously low.

"Relda, tell me about this sword," a golden-haired man said as he studied the blade. Sabrina recognized it immediately. It was a gift from Grandpa Basil, and it had hung over her grandmother's bed as long as the girls has known her.

"It's a samurai sword from Japan, Sir Kay," Granny explained. "It's Shinto Era—a shogun's blade. You can tell from the cherry blossoms carved into the steel. I think it's easily worth ten thousand dollars."

Sir Kay removed the sword from its hilt and examined it closely. "Is it enchanted?"

Granny shook her head. "I'm not selling anything magical today."

Sir Kay frowned. "How much are you asking for it?"

"Make me an offer."

"I'll give you a hundred bucks," Sir Kay said.

"That's ridiculous," Sabrina snapped.

Granny sighed. "Sold."

"Granny, no!" Sabrina cried. "You love that sword."

"It's just a sword, Sabrina," Granny replied.

Glinda the Good Witch came over carrying an umbrella stand

in the shape of an elephant foot. "I was hoping I'd see a few wands, Relda."

"Sorry, nothing magical today," the old woman said.

"Oh well, I'll take this," the witch said, disappointed. She handed Granny a ten-dollar bill and disappeared into the crowd.

"Mom, you're just giving this stuff away," Uncle Jake complained. He waved an old book in the air. "This is a signed edition of *Of Mice and Men*! The price tag says ten bucks. It's worth thousands!"

"You and your brother spilled fruit punch on it," Granny said. "Its value dropped dramatically."

Uncle Jake frowned and tossed the book onto a table, then turned to a crate of old records. "You're selling my Johnny Cash albums? These are priceless!"

"What would you have me do, Jacob? Do you want to lose the house?" Granny was suddenly so upset she was near tears.

"Granny, if it would help, I could set up a lemonade stand," Daphne offered as she gave the old woman a hug.

Granny pulled the little girl close. The embrace seemed to calm her. "That's a wonderful idea, Daphne."

"Yeah, if we sell each glass for thirty thousand dollars," Sabrina said under her breath. "Where's Charming?"

"He's keeping a low profile," Granny said, gesturing back to the house.

Sabrina spotted him peering through the living-room curtains.

Just then, a police car pulled up. Nottingham stepped out and stalked across the lawn. A white bandage was wrapped around his nose, and he was sporting two black eyes.

"Good morning, Sheriff," Granny said, trying to sound chipper.

"Selling your trash, are you, Grimm?" the sheriff sneered. "I doubt you could give most of this away."

"Well, you know what they say, one person's trash is another person's treasure," the old woman replied.

"You know what else they say? Ferryport Landing is a town for Everafters, not humans. This little sale of yours is not going to save your house." He picked up an African mask, flipped it over, then dropped it back to the table as if it were a wad of used tissue.

"Is there anything specific you're looking for today?" Granny asked.

"You don't happen to have any full-length mirrors do you?"

"Oh, no, not today."

Sabrina watched his face, terrified that he would recognize the girls from the night before. He was clearly looking for Charming's mirror. He might even have figured out its special secret.

"I notice you've had a little accident," Granny continued.

Nottingham's lip curled. "Yes . . . an accident."

"You need to be more careful."

"Thank you for your heartfelt advice," the sheriff seethed.

"Perhaps you'd be interested in a pair of sunglasses! No one would see your bruised eyes."

Nottingham sneered. "A clever suggestion, but no thanks. Perhaps I should buy a chair instead. It could be fun to watch your desperate little play. Though I know how it's going to end—in foreclosure."

Uncle Jake brought over a high-backed chair and set it down. "This one is twenty bucks."

Nottingham laughed. He paid Granny Relda and sat down.

"Money well spent," he sang.

He was grinning like it was his birthday when former deputies Boarman and Swineheart arrived. They were two of the Three Little Pigs, ex-police officers, and good friends to the Grimms.

"Hello, boys," Granny said. "Can I interest you in anything? We've got some great bargains here."

Boarman and Swineheart nodded, eyeing Nottingham warily. "How much money have you raised so far, Relda?" Swineheart asked.

"Oh, I think we've gotten a couple hundred dollars so far," the old woman said. "Not a bad start, really."

Sabrina cringed. The sale had been going on for four hours. They would never raise the full three hundred thousand dollars.

Boarman picked up a letter opener. Its marble handle was engraved with delicate roses. "This is beautiful," the portly man said.

"Yes, Basil bought that for me on our honeymoon in Paris," Granny said wistfully.

"I'll take it," Boarman said. He reached into his pocket and pulled out an enormous roll of money. He handed the whole thing to Granny Relda.

"Mr. Boarman, this is too much. The letter opener is only ten dollars," the old woman said.

Boarman smiled. "Is that so? I forgot my reading glasses this morning. It thought the price tag said ten thousand dollars. Oh well, keep the change."

Sabrina was stunned silent, as was nearly everyone else. Nottingham was so shocked he nearly fell out of his chair.

Swineheart selected a set of silver steak knives in an oak box. "These are lovely," he said, pressing an even bigger wad of cash into the old woman's hand. "I hope twenty-five thousand dollars is enough. I won't pay a penny more."

"What is the meaning of this?" Nottingham cried.

Before anyone could explain, Briar Rose appeared, along with a group of Everafters the family had known for years: Mr. Seven, Snow White, Geppetto, Morgan le Fay, King Arthur, and many more. They all gathered around Granny Relda.

"Oh, good. I was worried we'd get here too late and all the good stuff would be gone," Briar said, taking a glass paperweight off the table and handing the old woman an envelope overflowing with money.

"Briar, you don't have to do this," Uncle Jake said.

"I can't exactly date a guy who's homeless," she said with a wink.

"But this is too much," Granny said. "I can't accept this money. You're giving away a small fortune."

"No worries," Mr. Seven said as he approached the table. "We live in Ferryport Landing. What are we going to spend our money on anyway?"

The crowd of Everafters bought every little knickknack, paying ridiculous sums for each. With every sale, Nottingham threw a new fit. He fumed and raged and threatened everyone, but the sales continued.

As the girls watched from the porch, they heard a tapping behind them and realized Prince Charming was trying to get their attention.

"What are you doing? Why aren't you working on the case?" he demanded when they went in to see him.

"We're helping with the yard sale," Sabrina answered. "You know, we're only kids. It's not like we can just hop in a car and drive downtown."

"Not again, at least," Daphne said, reminding her sister of the time they drove Mr. Van Winkle's cab.

"Haven't you ever snuck out before? This is the perfect opportunity. Your grandmother is distracted. Take the magic detector and go! If she asks for you, I'll tell her you're upstairs fussing with your hair or playing dollies."

"Is that what you think we do with our free time?" Sabrina asked, shocked.

"Just go!"

The girls raced upstairs to retrieve the magic detector and nearly knocked over Puck in the hallway. He was nailing boards across his bedroom door.

"What are you doing?" Sabrina asked.

"There's hard work going on outside and I know at any moment someone is going to ask me to help, so I'm shutting myself up until the risk is gone. I'm very allergic to hard work," he said. "I once carried a box for the old woman, and I never recovered. How are you managing to avoid it?"

"Uh . . . we're just taking a break," Sabrina stammered.

"Do you smell that?" Puck asked.

"Smell what?" Daphne replied.

"A lie. I smell a lie, and it's stinky. C'mon, tell me the truth."

Sabrina knew the fairy would never give up, so she dragged him into her bedroom with her sister in tow. "We're still trying to solve the mystery of all those stolen magical items," Sabrina said.

"And you don't want the old lady or Canis to find out? Why?"

"They'll try to stop us," Daphne said.

"That's incredibly sneaky and dishonest," Puck said.

The girls nodded with shame.

"I'm proud of you," Puck said. "I want to help. We can sneak out of your bedroom window, and I'll fly you wherever you want."

"Maybe you want to change your pants first?" Daphne said.

Puck glanced down at his filthy jeans. "No. Why?"

"They don't fit you anymore."

Sabrina studied the boy's pants. Normally the cuffs dragged on the ground and into whatever Puck stomped through, but now they stopped several inches above his ankles.

"They must have shrunk in the wash," Puck said.

"Since when do you wash your clothes?"

Puck shrugged. "Are we going to do this or not?"

Daphne grabbed the magic detector from her bureau and slipped it into her pocket. Then she joined Sabrina and Puck at the window. Puck leaped out, flapping his wings to hover outside. He reached out for Sabrina first. She eyed his hand and paused. She would choose to hold that hand in the future. Thinking about it made her nervous and sweaty. *No!* She had to put all of it out of her mind. She snatched Puck's hand quickly before the boy noticed her hesitation, though she caught Daphne's grin out of the corner of her eye.

"Don't you say a word," Sabrina grumbled to her sister.

In no time, the trio was sailing high above the treetops, out of sight of their family and friends on the front lawn.

"Are you feeling anything?" Sabrina shouted over the wind.

Daphne shook her head. "Nothing at all."

"Remember what Charming said," Sabrina replied. "Concentrate on what we're looking for. Think about the clock and the wand and the water."

Daphne agreed and closed her eyes tightly.

"Are you concentrating on magic or passing gas?" Puck teased.

"Shut up," Daphne growled.

They flew over the train station and past the park, then past the shuttered elementary school. Once they were over Main Street, Daphne began to shimmer and vibrate.

"Hey! I'm picking up something," she said. "I can't explain why, but I feel like we should head toward the river."

Puck circled back and landed near the tiny marina, and Daphne led the rest of the way. The trio walked down the road while the little girl described the sensation of using the magic detector. The feeling got stronger as they walked, which was good, but Daphne was visibly, violently shaking, which was bad. Sabrina was worried someone might see them, but the streets were empty. It was like walking through a ghost town. The vibrations were stronger than ever as they reached Ms. Rose's coffee shop and the radio station across the street.

"Are you OK?" Puck asked as he watched the little girl turn into a blur.

"I'm all right," Daphne said. Her voice sounded like she was talking through an electric fan. "We're really close, but it's hard to pinpoint exactly where they are."

"All right, take a break," Sabrina said.

Daphne slipped the black marble into her pocket, and the vibrations stopped. "Thanks. I thought I was going to hurl."

The girls gazed through the windows of the Sacred Grounds coffee shop, then ducked down to avoid being spotted. Briar Rose and Snow White had left the yard sale and were sitting inside the café, along with Dr. Cindy and another woman with long, flowing red hair. Ms. White was in tears.

"Charming hasn't called her yet. He's being a jerk," Daphne said. "She's so worried about him, and he's just hiding in our house."

"I guess it's part of his plan to save her," Sabrina said.

"Let's go in and try to cheer her up."

"No way. We've got magic to find, and I'm not going anywhere near no blubbering female," Puck said.

"He's gross, but he makes a fair point. We're wasting time," Sabrina said. "We need to keep looking for the stolen items."

"I don't care," Daphne declared. "Ms. White is my friend."

"I won't go!" Puck cried.

"They have muffins," Daphne said.

"Then let's go," he said, pushing past the girls into the café.

"You can get him to do anything if you offer him food," Daphne said. "He's kind of like a dog."

The girls entered the coffee shop and crossed the room to greet the four women.

"Hello," Daphne said.

"Oh, hello, girls," Snow said, as she hurried to dry her tears on a napkin. "Are you here by yourselves? It's not safe to be in the streets on your own."

"It's all right," Puck said, pointing to his wooden sword. "I brought Mr. Stabby."

"What's wrong, Ms. White?" Daphne asked.

"Snow is having a difficult day," Cindy explained.

"I'm just worried about Billy," the teacher said with a sniffle.

Sabrina and Daphne shared a look.

"He's fine," Sabrina said. "I mean, I'm sure he's fine."

"That's what I've been telling her," the fourth woman said. Red hair framed her creamy complexion and green eyes. To Sabrina she looked like a glamorous star from an old movie. "You must be Henry's girls. I've been eager to meet you. I'm Rapunzel."

Daphne let out a squeal.

"She does that for everyone?" Cindy asked with a laugh. "I thought I was special."

"Snow, William doesn't deserve your tears, girlfriend," Rapunzel said.

"She's right, Snow," Ms. Rose said. "Whenever his pride is

hurt, he runs off—hunting, he used to call it, but I knew better. He was sulking. This is no different. Losing the election hurt his fragile ego."

"William does have his childish moments," Cindy added. "I was married to the man for nearly a hundred years. He'd throw tantrums, disappear, and then show up again without any explanation. He'll be back."

"We've all seen it before, Snow," Rapunzel said.

"But he's been gone for two months. I can't believe he hasn't called or written. Why won't he let me know he's OK?" Ms. White sobbed.

Rapunzel sighed. "You thought you were different."

Snow wiped her eyes. "What?"

"You thought that because you two reunited after five hundred years your love was special. I thought the same thing. He swept me away. I thought we had our happily ever after, too."

"The thing is . . ." Cindy said, "she *is* special."

Rapunzel and Briar Rose shifted uncomfortably.

"I knew it, even when we were married," Cindy continued. "She was the one. We're all amazing women: beautiful, smart, capable. But none of us are Snow White."

"Oh, Cindy. Don't," Ms. White said.

"I'm not angry, Snow. I'm over that, but I understand people. I had a family that was completely nuts. I was married to a guy who was more boy than man. Even my fairy godmother was off her rocker. I know the truth when it's looking me in the face. William never got over you. It's why I left him."

Sabrina looked to Ms. Rose, then Rapunzel. They were both nodding.

"William always loved you," Briar Rose said. "Not that he didn't try to love me, or Rapunzel. He tried to be a good husband to each of us, but his heart was always yours. You're his soul mate."

"And he's yours," Rapunzel added. "I never understood why you left him at the altar."

"We were too young. It was all happening so fast," Ms. White explained.

"I wish I had been that smart," Rapunzel said.

Briar Rose shook her head. "No, you don't."

Rapunzel laughed. "You're right. It was fun while it lasted."

Cindy reached over and took Ms. White's hand. "For a long time I resented you, Snow. Your spirit hung over our home like a ghost. Occasionally, we would be at a party and hear about something that was going on in your life, and his eyes would fix on whoever was saying it. For days he would be distant, distracted. He'd spend a week at the stables, claiming the horses needed attention, but I wasn't stupid."

"Is this true?" Ms. White asked, looking at the other women in the group. They all nodded. "I'm sorry."

"Don't be. I adore you, and if not for you I would never had met Tom. He's all the prince I will ever need. What I'm trying to say to you is I'm a little worried about Billy. His love for you is so endless. If he hasn't contacted you, I have to think he's in some kind of trouble."

"There goes Dr. Cindy," Rapunzel said. "Could you turn off the honesty you give your callers and remember we're trying to cheer this woman up?"

"Ms. White, I bet he's going to pop up any day now," Daphne said. "And he'll have a crazy story, which you should believe, and it will explain everything."

"I hope you're right," Ms. White said.

"Well, when he does, I hope you give him a karate kick to the behind," Briar Rose said, which caused the four women to burst into laughter.

"Briar, I swear, you don't say much, but when you do it's hilarious," Rapunzel said. "Girls, how about we make this a regular thing?"

The women glanced at one another hesitantly.

"I don't know," Cindy said.

"Come on!" Rapunzel cried. "We've been avoiding each other in this silly little town for two hundred years! Let's put it all behind us, meet for brunch, start a book club, gossip. Let's be friends!"

"What if we played poker?" Briar Rose suggested.

Snow threw up her arms. "How are Tuesday nights?"

"Oh, this sounds like trouble," Dr. Cindy said. "But I'm in!"

"Can I come?" Daphne asked.

The table roared with laughter. "Of course. We'll take anyone's money," Ms. White said, and the women laughed again.

"Tuesday nights at my place. I'll make something decadent that we shouldn't eat. We'll call ourselves the Poker Princesses," Rapunzel said.

Puck came over with a sack of muffins. "What's all the commotion?"

"And no boys!" Briar Rose cried. The Poker Princesses applauded.

Puck grumbled and stormed out of the coffee shop. Sabrina grabbed her sister, said good-bye, and chased after the fairy.

"We should get back," Sabrina said as they left. "Granny is going to miss us."

Daphne nodded. "I think we've done all we can, anyway. At least we know the stolen stuff is on this block. Now we need a way to find their exact location."

Oddly enough, Granny hadn't missed them. Three quarters of the items from the yard sale were sold, and their grandmother was counting a huge stack of bills. Nottingham was long gone, and the crowds had disappeared as well. Puck rushed up to his room for fear of being drafted into helping put things away. Sabrina heard him working on his barricade again.

"Oh, hello, girls," Granny said. "As they say in the business world, we made a killing."

"Enough to pay the taxes?" Daphne asked.

Granny Relda nodded. "I think that should put to rest the idea that all the Everafters hate us. If you two can help Mr. Canis bring what's left back into the house, then we can go down and pay the bill. It will be nice to have this off my shoulders."

The children helped put everything back in its original place. The house seemed emptier. Paintings were gone, as was the overstuffed chair in the living room. Most of the rugs and kitchen utensils had been sold, including the toaster and the coffeepot. Daphne was heartbroken when she discovered Granny had sold the ice-cream scoop, but the old woman said she was tired of all the clutter anyway. She claimed a yard sale was long overdue.

Charming's magic mirror was leaning against a wall in the living room. It warped and shimmied as the prince stepped through the reflection. He sported a fresh shave and haircut, and he had swapped Uncle Jake's jeans for a stylish black suit. Apparently, the Hotel of Wonders lived up to its reputation as a full-service establishment.

"Swanky," Daphne said.

"Perhaps later you'll give me a tour of your mirror," Granny Relda said. "I've never been inside any but our own."

Charming nodded. "Perhaps."

"Well, I suppose I should go and fetch Mr. Canis and Jacob," Granny said as she hurried upstairs. "We've got the tax money. Oh, I do so hope it ruins Mayor Heart's day."

When she was gone, Charming turned to the children.

"What did you find?" he asked.

"Whoever has the stolen items has got them stashed somewhere near Briar Rose's coffee shop. We were picking up crazy vibes but couldn't find the exact location."

"Mucho huge-o vibes. I need more practice to get more specific," Daphne added, and then her tone turned angry. "We also saw Ms. White."

"Oh. How is she?" Charming asked.

"Heartbroken! She thinks you're dead."

Charming lowered his eyes. "It can't be helped."

"She's a mess," Sabrina said. "Can't you send her a note? She'd feel better if you let her know you're OK."

"I can't," he said.

"I think we can trust her with what we know, and—"

"Stop!" Charming shouted. "I thought you understood. I don't want her to suffer, but to save her life I have to do drastic things!"

"Drastic things?"

"Never mind," the prince mumbled. "She'll be all right. I'd rather her have a broken heart than one that doesn't beat at all."

"Fine," Sabrina said, throwing her hands up. Daphne frowned but didn't argue, and the conversation came to a halt when Granny returned with Mr. Canis and Uncle Jake. The old man's anger at Charming was as visible as it had been the night before.

"Who wants to see the mayor's head pop off?" Granny asked. "Want to come with us to the tax office?"

"I wouldn't miss that for the world." Sabrina smiled.

Uncle Jake reached into his pocket and pulled out a camera. "I'm taking pictures!"

"William, would you mind keeping an eye on the house while we're gone?" the old woman asked.

"Do you think it is wise to leave him here alone?" Canis demanded before Charming could answer.

Granny flushed. "Mr. Canis!"

"Are you afraid I will rob you blind?" Charming asked.

"I wouldn't put anything past you," Canis said, stepping close to the prince.

"Gentlemen! That's enough!" Granny said firmly.

Canis growled and stormed outside. Granny followed, as did the girls.

"That was entirely uncalled for!" Granny shouted.

"Having him in the house is entirely uncalled for!" Canis yelled back.

Sabrina and Daphne were shocked. Even when Mr. Canis and Granny had fought the last few days, the girls had never heard the old man raise his voice at her. In a world filled with people Mr. Canis couldn't stand, Granny Relda had always earned his utmost respect.

"I know the two of you have your history," Granny said, "but the man is homeless."

"That man deserves no better than to be homeless."

"It is not in my habit to turn away a person in need," Granny said.

"Then you are a fool!" Canis declared.

"Was I a fool when I took you in?" Granny snapped back. "Even my husband told me you were untrustworthy, but I turned a deaf ear. And you have become my dearest friend and my most trusted companion."

They got into the family's ancient car. It roared, spit, and knocked violently. Canis threw the old jalopy into reverse and whipped out into the street. When he put it into drive, the engine screamed like a cat in a bathtub. He ignored its protests and stomped on the accelerator. Granny gave him a scolding look, but the two did not speak to each other again.

The crowd of protesters from the day before was gone from the courthouse steps. Only a few stragglers remained, and they looked even more desperate than they had earlier. The security guard they'd met the day before was standing in the same spot. He seemed surprised to see the family. They waved at him and continued down the hallway to the tax office. Once inside, Granny rang the bell for service.

"I really can't wait to see her face," Granny said softly.

It wasn't long before Mayor Heart came around the corner. She spotted the family and gasped. "What are you doing here?"

"We've come to pay our taxes, of course," Granny said, setting a bag of money on the countertop.

The woman snatched her megaphone and raised it to her mouth. "THAT'S NOT POSSIBLE! NOTTINGHAM!" she shouted, then slammed the device down on the countertop so hard, Sabrina thought it might break.

"Someone's having a bad day," Daphne said with a grin.

Seconds later, Sheriff Nottingham hobbled into the room. "What is it, woman? Don't you know I have my hands full? The phone is ringing off the hook. Apparently some fool in a civil war uniform is over on Applebee's farm firing a musket!"

"The Grimms have come to pay their taxes . . . AGAIN!" Heart said, gesturing wildly at the family.

The sheriff nodded, but his face was dark and angry. "I know."

"It's all there, Mayor, and like before I'm going to need a receipt," Granny Relda said.

"You're enjoying this!" Heart shouted.

"What? Paying taxes? I doubt there are too many people who enjoy it," Granny said.

"Well, you can come in here with a million dollars next time and it won't change anything. I want you out of this town, Relda Grimm—you and your filthy brood. I want every human out of Ferryport Landing, and I always get what I want."

Suddenly, the door flew open and one of the playing-card guards raced inside.

"Sheriff, we've got a situation!" he yelled.

"Calm yourself, you idiot!"

"There's a ship coming up the river," the guard said. "It looks pretty old."

"So what?" Nottingham said. "Ships come up and down the river every day."

"This one has cannons mounted on it," the guard said.

"Cannons?" Granny repeated.

Just then, the walkie-talkie strapped to the guard's waist squawked. "Seven of Clubs, you're not going to believe this ship. There must be a thousand people on it, and they're all dressed like they're going to a costume party. Plus, you gotta see this storm. It just came out of nowhere. Wait a minute . . . I think

the boat has a name painted on the side. It looks German . . .
Neuer Anfang."

"*New Beginning,*" Granny translated.

"It can't be!" Mayor Heart shouted.

Nottingham leaped over the counter dividing the room and
pushed past the family as he raced out the door. Mayor Heart was
hot on his heels.

"What?" Sabrina cried. "What's the big deal about this ship?"

"The *New Beginning* was the name of the ship the Brothers
Grimm used to bring the Everafters to America," Uncle Jake said.

Mr. Canis was already out of the car and hurrying to join them
when they exited the courthouse. "Have you heard the news?"

Granny nodded. "Yes. It must be some kind of prank."

"It's not," Canis said. "I'll never forget the smell of that boat.
Relda, it's the real thing—but how?"

The family charged down the street as quickly as they could.
By the time they reached the marina, there was a huge crowd of
people gathered there. The Grimms pushed through the mob until they got to the front. There it was: a massive ship with several
white sails fluttering in an angry wind. Hovering over the ship was
a swirling black storm—another tear in time—which was rapidly
vanishing. A tiny rowboat was already cruising toward the shore
with a lone man at the oars.

"Who is it?" Daphne wondered, looking across the river.

Granny reached into her huge handbag and took out a pair of binoculars. "Oh dear," she said.

"What? Who is it?" Sabrina asked.

Granny handed her the binoculars. Sabrina peered through the lenses, adjusting them to focus first on the ship. The deck was filled with princes, princesses, witches, ogres, dwarves, and numerous hairy and feathered creatures. She then searched the water for the rowboat. A man with brown hair and a rather large nose was approaching the shore. He seemed oddly familiar, as if she had seen a picture of him before, or maybe a drawing . . . Then it dawned on her.

"Granny, is that who I think it is?"

"Yes, Sabrina. That's your great-great-great-great-grandfather, Wilhelm Grimm," Granny said.

9

THE LITTLE ROWBOAT DRIFTED TO THE SHORE, and its occupant climbed on land. He was shorter than Sabrina expected, wearing a long brown coat and a wide-brimmed hat. His eyes were quite small and almost black. He turned and gazed at the crowd with awe.

"*Ist das Amerika?*" Wilhelm asked.

"*Ja, das ist Amerika. Willkommen, Wilhelm. Willkommen,*" Granny said.

"What did you just say?" Daphne asked.

"I just welcomed him to America," Granny said, then turned back to Wilhelm. "Do you speak English?"

"*Ja,* a little," Wilhelm said. "Is this New York?"

Granny nodded.

Wilhelm scanned the curious crowd once more. When he spotted Briar Rose, he rushed to her. Confused and excited, he took her hands, then looked back at his ship. "*Wie sind Sie hier herkommen? Waren Sie auf dem Schiff?*" he asked.

"What is he saying?" Daphne asked.

"He's confused," Granny explained.

"How can you be here?" Wilhelm turned and pointed at the ship. "And there?"

Before anyone could explain, Nottingham pulled handcuffs from his coat and clamped them around Wilhelm's wrists. "Ask him if he understands he's under arrest."

Nottingham marched Wilhelm toward the town jail, while the little man cried out in protest. Granny followed, demanding that the sheriff release Wilhelm and doing her best to calm her bewildered ancestor. She instructed the girls to stay with Mr. Canis.

"I'm on that boat," Briar Rose said as Uncle Jake took her hand. "I mean, I was on that boat. I mean . . . I don't know what I mean."

"How did this happen?" Mr. Seven asked.

Sabrina and Daphne looked at each other. They knew, sort of, how it had happened. They just didn't know who or what was causing it to happen. Apparently, their conspiratorial look wasn't lost on Mr. Canis. He snatched them each by an arm and dragged them away from the crowd.

"You know something," he accused the girls.

Sabrina did her best to play innocent. She glanced over at Daphne, who was whipping her head around, trying to avoid the old man's eyes.

"I don't know what you're talking about," Sabrina mumbled.

"Child, this is no time for lies," Canis growled.

"We promised Mr. Charming that we wouldn't say anything," Daphne blurted out. Sabrina scowled. Daphne was no good at lying.

Canis bristled. "I should have known he had something to do with this."

"You've got it wrong, Mr. Canis," Sabrina said, throwing her hands up in surrender. "He's trying to help."

"Help who?"

"It's going to sound crazy."

"Try me," the hulking man said. Sabrina looked up into his face. She saw his wolflike features, more distinct every day. If anyone would believe the story she was about to tell it would be him.

"It's a tear in time," Sabrina said. "It's been happening all over town, but this is the biggest incident yet."

"A tear in what?"

"In time. Things are slipping out of the future and the past and popping up in places where they don't belong."

"And how do you know this?"

"Because we did it ourselves," Daphne said. "Yesterday when you took us out tracking, we didn't get lost in the forest. We went to the future!"

"How does Charming have anything to do with this?" Canis asked impatiently.

"He got stuck there, too, right after the election," Daphne said. "He was trapped for months and trying to find a way back."

"Why haven't you told anyone?" Canis asked.

"We know things . . . about the future, things we're trying to change. If we tell everyone what we know, then things might change in ways we can't expect. We all agreed to keep what we know to ourselves just to be safe."

"What is so bad about the future that needs to be changed?" Canis demanded.

"We can't tell you," Sabrina cried.

"It's something about me, isn't it?"

A tear rolled down Daphne's cheek. "Please don't make us tell, Mr. Canis," she begged.

Canis looked shaken but didn't press the girls further.

"You can't tell anyone you know this, not even Granny," Sabrina said.

"Very well. At least tell me how to stop these time tears," Canis asked.

"We don't know. Honest!" Daphne said, as she took out her magic detector. "But we've got something that helps us find them. I'm just not very good at using it yet."

"Plus, we think we know what's causing them. The stolen enchanted items we've been investigating were combined to make a brand new kind of magic. Whoever stole them is causing the tears," Sabrina explained as best she could. "When we went to the future we learned that we never solved this case. If we find the crook and stop this magic, we'll not only stop the tears, but change the future, too."

Just then, a fiery explosion erupted in the water. When Sabrina searched for the source of the attack she noticed that one of the cannons on the ship had a trail of smoke drifting out of it.

"They're firing on us!" Sabrina exclaimed.

"Of course they are; we just arrested their captain," Canis said, rushing back to the dock. "Those aren't pebbles they're throwing at you, people. Get back!"

Another cannonball hit the marina. Wood and splinters blasted in every direction.

"Are we going to stand here and let them attack?" King Arthur shouted as he stepped through the crowd. "Shouldn't we fire back?"

"No! We could accidentally wipe out our own existence," a jowly man said from the crowd. Sabrina thought at first that he was elderly, but then she realized his wrinkled skin wasn't skin at all but an old burlap sack. He had straw sticking out of his cuffs, and he wore an old farmer's hat on his head.

"What are you talking about, Scarecrow?" Mr. Seven shouted.

"That ship has sailed here from the past. How and why, I can't say, but I do know one thing: if you attack it, the consequences will be dire. Many of you are onboard, or rather, a version of you from two hundred years ago. If you fire on them, you could accidentally kill yourself."

"Scarecrow, I never can make heads or tails of anything you say," one of the Three Blind Mice complained. "Are you sure the Wizard gave you brains? I get the feeling he stuffed your head with cotton candy."

"You've got a lot of nerve. If you only had a brain you might still have a tail," the Scarecrow replied.

"Stop arguing," Canis commanded. "Scarecrow, are you saying that if someone on that ship is killed, it could kill them now?"

The Scarecrow nodded. "Absolutely, as well as a chain of events no one could predict. Let's say someone killed King Arthur. He would cease to exist immediately, and everything he's done since arriving in this town would never have happened, either. Every person he's met, every job he's held—it would all be different, and it could warp the present into something we might not even recognize, depending upon who died in such a foolish attack."

In a flash, Canis snatched the girls in his arms and ran up the street, with one Grimm slung over each shoulder.

"What are you doing?" Sabrina yelled.

"Nottingham's got Wilhelm!" he shouted. "If he's got half the brains the Scarecrow does, he's likely to figure out that killing Wilhelm might change a lot of things around here. Killing him would destroy the barrier that traps us in this town and also put an end to all of his descendants. Every member of your family would cease to exist, including the two of you."

"Fudge," Daphne mumbled.

Sabrina looked back at the crowd by the river. As she watched, many of the bystanders began chasing after them. It seemed they now understood the dark opportunity Canis had just explained, too. "Uh, could you run a little faster?" she asked.

The jailhouse was a mob scene. There were hundreds of Everafters outside, demanding answers about the arrival of the *New Beginning*. Canis and pushed people aside as he forced his way into the tiny building. Once inside, they found Granny at the front desk, pounding on the table and calling out for the sheriff.

"Where is Wilhelm?" Canis asked, setting the girls down.

"Nottingham took him back to a cell for interrogation," she said.

"I have a feeling his definition of the word interrogation is different than ours," Canis said. "We have to get him out of there."

Granny nodded.

Then the sheriff stepped back into the lobby. He wore a grin like a little boy who has just gotten a bicycle for his birthday.

"Sheriff Nottingham!" Granny exclaimed. "You had no right to arrest that man."

"I have every right. I'm the sheriff," he said.

"What is his crime?"

"Let's see. He doesn't have a sailing license, or a passport, and he's trying to sneak foreigners into the country."

"He doesn't belong here, Nottingham," Canis said.

"Oh, I'm well aware he doesn't belong here," Nottingham said. "To be honest, I've ignored all the bizarre reports that came in this week. Lenni Lenape Indian tribes, dinosaurs, Civil War soldiers—I thought everyone was losing their minds. Now I see that time has been coughing up all kinds of surprises, and it saved the biggest one for me. That man back there is a gift!"

"Gift! What are you talking about?" Granny demanded.

"I'm going to be a hero, Mrs. Grimm. With one slash of my dagger, I will end two hundred years of suffering for this entire town."

"You can't just kill a man," Sabrina said. "You're a police officer."

Nottingham laughed. "Child, do you think I took this job because I care about justice? Oh, how I will miss you silly people. I wonder if I'll remember you when it's all said and done. It would be a shame if I didn't."

"You won't," Granny Relda said. "And neither will anyone else. Not even a little. So, if you plan to erase my family, you should put on a show of it. Schedule a public execution. Make it a spectacle."

"Granny, what are you doing?" Sabrina was stunned by the old woman's suggestion.

"Midnight tonight!" a voice shouted through a megaphone. The crowd parted, and Mayor Heart stepped through. "Tonight I make good on my campaign promise of changing everything. I bet you didn't guess just how much change I had planned. It's going to be quite a celebration, folks. Everyone is invited."

She let out a wicked laugh as she glared at the Grimm family. "Aren't you going to tell us we'll never get away with this?"

The crowd roared with laughter.

"I thought it was understood," Granny Relda said calmly. She took the girls by the hand and led them through the masses and out into the street. Uncle Jake was waiting by the car when they arrived.

"Is he in there?" he asked, pointing back toward the jail.

Granny nodded. "Heaven only knows how he got here."

Sabrina, Daphne, and Mr. Canis shared a look but kept quiet.

"What are we going to do, Mom?" Uncle Jake asked.

"Heart and Nottingham want Wilhelm dead. I just bought us six hours to come up with a plan to save him," she said. "In the meantime, we should hurry home. We need to rally the troops."

"You want to what?" Uncle Jake said, leaping from his seat on the family couch.

"I want you to tell Baba Yaga that Nottingham has her wand," Granny said.

Charming, Canis, Sabrina, Daphne, Puck, and even Elvis seemed shocked by Granny's plan. They gazed at one another in disbelief.

"You want to lie to her?" Uncle Jake asked. "The only reason she respects you is because she trusts you."

"We're going to need her as a distraction," the old woman explained. "If she thinks the sheriff has her wand, she'll attack the police station to get it back. Nottingham will be so busy trying to stay alive he won't hear Mr. Canis knocking down the back wall to free Wilhelm."

Puck clapped his hands. "A jailbreak. I love it!"

Uncle Jake, however, stood shaking his head. "If we lie to Baba Yaga, things will get ugly, and we'll never be able to go to her for help ever again. Not that I'll miss her all that much, but it's nice to know we have her in our back pocket when things are desperate."

"Things are already desperate," Charming said.

"I understand the consequences," the old woman said, "but the alternative is much worse. Saving Wilhelm isn't just about saving this family; it could mean saving the entire world."

"Agreed," Jake said. "I just wish I didn't have to be the one to lie to her."

"What are you complaining about? You have the cool job," Puck said.

"Puck, your job is the most important," Granny said.

"Except it doesn't include magical attacks and explosions," Puck complained.

"What about us?" Daphne asked as she rubbed Elvis's chin. The big dog watched Granny Relda attentively as if waiting to be given a job as well.

"You and Sabrina are sticking close to me. I may need your help getting Wilhelm to safety," Granny said.

"But there's a problem with your plan, General," Charming said.

"General?" Granny Relda said.

"I mean . . . what are you going to do with Wilhelm once he's safe? You won't be able to hide him in this town. Nottingham is going to know who was responsible."

Granny shook her head. "In all honesty I don't know. We'll have to get him back on the *New Beginning* with the others. His brother Jacob is on the ship, as well. They will have to flee, go somewhere far from here and hope they sail back into one of these time storms.

"I suggest you all have something to eat and get some rest. This is probably going to be the longest night of our lives," she said, rubbing her tired face.

Everyone ate in silence. When dinner was finished, Granny retired to her bedroom, Puck went to his room to prepare, Uncle Jake went off to find Baba Yaga, and Charming retreated into his mirror, leaving Mr. Canis and the girls alone.

The old man sat quietly. It seemed as if he was wrestling with a question. Sabrina knew what it would be and dreaded having to answer it.

"I lose control, don't I?"

"Mr. Canis—"

"Just tell me," he insisted.

Daphne nodded. Sabrina couldn't blame her. The old man deserved to know the truth.

"Can I do anything to stop it?" Mr. Canis finally asked, looking down at the sharp black claws on his hand.

"Of course!" Daphne said. "There has to be a way."

Sabrina, on the other hand, wasn't so sure. Canis had been creeping toward a complete metamorphosis ever since his fight with Jack the Giant Killer. No amount of yoga and meditation made a difference, and every day he seemed more and more wolflike. Still, she kept her doubts to herself and chose to be hopeful. "We have already changed a few things. Maybe you can, too."

Canis looked defeated. He got up from his chair and repeated Granny Relda's advice about getting some rest. He slowly climbed the steps to his room, the floorboards groaning under his tremendous weight.

"I've got a bad feeling," Sabrina said.

"About tonight?" Daphne asked.

"No, about the future. We still haven't found the missing items, and it seems like things keep popping up to get in the way. What if we don't catch the crook? What if we don't solve this mystery? What if there are things we can't change?"

Sabrina awoke to the bed shaking violently. She looked over at Daphne and found her concentrating hard with her eyes closed tight. The magic detector was in her hand, and it was vibrating powerfully.

"What's going on?" Sabrina asked.

"I feel a time tear opening. Ugh, I might barf," Daphne groaned.

"Can you tell where it's going to happen?"

"In the river, I think. It's going to be a big one, too."

"Big enough for Wilhelm's ship?"

"Mucho big-o!" Daphne slipped the black marble into her pocket, and the shaking stopped. "We have to go now!"

Sabrina glanced over at the alarm clock.

"It's only ten o'clock. We can't go now. What about Uncle Jake? We don't know if he's found Baba Yaga yet!"

"This could be our only chance to send Wilhelm and the ship back where they belong," Daphne said as she leaped out of bed.

The girls raced into their grandmother's room. Granny Relda was lying in bed wide awake.

"*Lieblings*, for heaven's sake!" Granny Relda cried.

"There's a time tear opening in the river. We need to go now."

"A time what?" the old woman said.

"A hole in time," Sabrina explained. "We need to get Wilhelm out of jail and back on the boat, now!"

"Girls, how do you know all this?"

"Granny, you keep secrets from us sometimes to protect us, right?" Daphne asked.

The old woman nodded.

"Well, this is our secret, and you're just going to have to trust us, like we trust you."

Granny laughed. "But, girls, you never trust me."

"Fine, then trust us like we're supposed to trust you," Sabrina said, pulling her grandmother out of bed and down the hallway. Meanwhile, Daphne pounded on Puck's door. The fairy joined them shortly, strapped with enough of his glop grenades to fight a war.

"Let's do this," he said.

Everyone rushed downstairs. Canis was sitting on the couch, ready to go.

"I heard the news," he replied. "The car is already warmed up."

"What about Jacob?" Charming asked as he poked his head out of his mirror.

"There's no way to reach him," Granny Relda said.

Charming vanished into the reflection but returned moments later, leading a brilliant white stallion through the portal. Even Canis, who was rarely surprised by anything, was stunned. Elvis looked up at the horse as if he were in the presence of royalty.

Daphne looked over at her grandmother with a smile. "Remember when you told me I couldn't have a pony because we didn't have enough room?"

Granny shook her head. "Not a chance."

"I'll go for Jacob," Charming said as he led the horse outside. The prince mounted his horse and raced off into the night without another word.

Mr. Canis whipped the old car through the empty back roads, over the wooden bridges, and across the abandoned train tracks like he was a race-car driver. Sabrina was happy he understood the urgency of their plan, but it was at times like this she wished the car had more modern safety features. She tightened the makeshift seat belt around her waist and said a silent prayer. For once, even Puck buckled up.

Canis parked across from the police station, and everyone got out.

"Puck, take your position," Granny said.

Puck's wings spread out and flapped vigorously, lifting him

into the air. "I'll wait for you at the dock," he said, then zipped off toward the river.

Canis nodded. "What next?"

"Unfortunately, this plan of ours was somewhat dependent upon Jacob," Granny said. "We need to give Charming some time to find him and Baba Yaga."

"We can't wait another second," Daphne said as she pointed to the sky. The stars had been devoured by a swirling black mass hovering high over the town. It was bigger and uglier than any of the previous storms. "We've got to do this now, Granny."

"All right," their grandmother said. "I suppose we can sneak around the back and knock a hole in the wall. At least that much of the plan could still work."

"No, stop!" Mr. Canis said, sniffing the air. "There are card guards stationed on the top of the building and a large group of them at the back."

"How many, do you think?" Granny said.

"I smell fifty in all."

"They knew we were coming," Sabrina said, spotting one of the playing-card guards peering over the edge of the jailhouse roof. She also saw the deadly broadsword he held in his hands.

"The three of you should wait here," Canis said.

"Old friend, you'll never get past them all. We need to try something different." Granny sighed.

"Like what?" Daphne asked.

"We'll go right through the front door," Sabrina said.

The family turned to her.

"Remember our escape training?" Sabrina said. "We kept getting caught because we were trying to be sneaky and Puck knew it. He knew we'd try to hide in the woods and was ready for us. We only managed to beat him when we did something he never expected. I bet you a million bucks Nottingham thinks we'll try something sneaky, too. He's put all his men at the back of the building assuming we'll try to go in that way, but he's not expecting us to go through the front door."

"Sabrina, that's brilliant. I bet the offices aren't guarded at all."

Suddenly, Mr. Canis started across the street. "Let's do it."

"What's the plan?" Granny asked as the rest of the family followed.

"I'll charge through and you follow," he said, then bolted right through the front door. He slammed through the offices like a wrecking ball, plowing through walls, overturning desks, and making his own path to the jail cells at the back of the building. The Grimms followed as well as they could, dodging falling plaster and torn electrical wires. They held their shirts over their faces to keep from breathing in the dust and debris. The blitz made a tremendous racket and would surely attract the attention of the guards soon, but Sabrina's theory was right. Nottingham hadn't bothered to fortify the front of the jail. There wasn't a single guard on duty.

They found Wilhelm locked inside a small cell. The poor man was terrified by the destruction he heard marching toward him and waved his chair threateningly at the group.

"*Zurück bleiben! Ich möchte Sie nicht verletzen!*" Wilhelm shouted.

"What did he say?" Sabrina asked.

"He's frightened. He thinks we've come to hurt him," Granny explained, then turned to the man. "Wilhelm, it's us. We've come to rescue you."

"Rescue?" Wilhelm cried. He set his chair down and shook his jail cell bars as if to remind them of their next obstacle.

Using his incredible strength, Canis pried the bars apart, bending them until there was an opening big enough for Wilhelm to step through.

Just then, Sabrina heard Nottingham's angry voice. "The prisoner is escaping, you fools! Go around to the front and stop him!" he shouted. His furious bellowing was followed by the approaching feet of what sounded like dozens of guards.

"We've got to get out of here—now," Granny said.

Canis stepped to the back wall, pulled back his fist, and slammed it into the concrete. It crumbled, shaking the rafters. A few cinder blocks completely collapsed, exposing the outdoors

to the group. One more hit sent a spray of concrete all over the room, but when the dust settled, there was a hole big enough for a seven-foot, three-hundred-pound man to step through.

"Everyone out!" Granny cried as she helped Sabrina and Daphne through the hole. She followed with Wilhelm.

Before Mr. Canis could get through, Sabrina heard a sinister voice from inside the station.

"You do realize that breaking a prisoner out of jail is a big no-no," Nottingham said, and then she heard Mr. Canis roar in pain. She couldn't see clearly what was happening, but she knew her friend was hurt. A moment later, Nottingham stepped through the hole.

"I really should arrest you, Grimms, but I have a better way of solving our problem," he said as he reached for the crossbow strapped to his back. He loaded it with a steel arrow and leveled it at Wilhelm's chest. "One shot changes everything in this town, and though I know the throngs of people eager to see Wilhelm swing from the gallows will be disappointed, having their freedom will more than make up for missing the show."

And then he pulled the trigger, and the arrow flew.

10

ITT SEEMED TO SABRINA THAT THE ARROW SAILED across space in slow motion. In that long moment she wondered what it would be like to suddenly not exist. Everything she had ever experienced would never have happened at all. Would it hurt, or would she just blink into nothing?

But the arrow never reached its target. A loud, quaking thump knocked everyone to the ground, and the deadly missile sailed over Wilhem. When they scrambled to their feet, the group was confronted with the source of the tiny earthquake. Baba Yaga had arrived in her horrifying house. The old crone was leaning out of her window with a glowing ball in her hand.

"I want my wand!" she shouted at Nottingham.

"I have no idea what you mean, your miserable old hag!" the sheriff raged.

A blast of red energy hit Nottingham in the chest and tossed him several yards before he crashed to the ground. Somehow, he had the presence of mind to dash behind a tree before the witch's house charged at him. One of its horrible, clawed legs snatched the tree out of the ground, roots and all, leaving the sheriff exposed and panicked.

Wilhelm cried out something in German, but his message was clear. Sabrina's great-great-great-great-grandfather was completely freaked out.

"I was too late," Charming said as he rode up on his stallion.

Uncle Jake was right behind him, hovering on a flying carpet. "We should go. Baba Yaga's not going to be fooled for very long, and when she figures out our lie she'll turn on us."

"We can't leave! Mr. Canis is still in there, and he's hurt!" Sabrina cried, pointing to the crumbling jailhouse.

Just then the old man stepped through the rubble. He held his hand to his left eye as blood seeped down his hairy wrist.

"Old friend!" Granny gasped.

"It is nothing," Canis said, but his voice was pained.

Granny removed a handkerchief from her handbag and gave it to him. He held it to his wound and then ushered everyone toward the marina. "Don't worry about me. We have to get Wilhelm to the boat."

The family raced the three blocks to the river. There they found Puck waiting impatiently.

"It's about time!" Puck cried.

"Sorry, Puck. We had an unexpected snag in our plan. Is the rowboat ready?" the old woman asked.

"Naturally," Puck replied.

Uncle Jake helped Granny Relda into it, then the girls, Wilhelm, and finally he climbed in himself.

"You know what to do?" Uncle Jake asked the fairy boy.

"You think I need help remembering how to cause trouble?" Puck crowed as he shot into the sky. He was barely aloft when a cannon was fired and the ball nearly knocked him out of the sky.

"They're shooting at us!" Daphne exclaimed.

"Duh!" Puck cried as he soared higher and higher.

Uncle Jake took the oars and rowed with all his might. The little boat streaked across the river, while cannonballs slammed into the water all around them.

"This big rescue mission is going to be for nothing if Wilhelm's ship sinks us," Sabrina said.

Wilhelm leaped from his seat and waved at the boat. His excitement nearly capsized them, and Sabrina braced herself to keep from falling in the river. His wild gestures made her nervous. He was making them an easier target.

Two more shots followed, one close enough to cause water to splash into the boat, but then the explosions stopped. They had smooth sailing the rest of the way to the ship. Uncle Jake and

Wilhelm helped Granny aboard, and then the girls scrambled up as well.

Sabrina was stunned by the people there to greet them. Nearly everyone she'd ever met from the town was there: Briar Rose; Mr. Seven and the other six dwarves; Ms. White; Beauty and her husband, the Beast; and even some old enemies like Jack the Giant Killer and Rumpelstiltskin. She stepped in front of her family and clenched her fists, fully prepared to fight her way off the ship, but then it dawned on her that no one knew who they were.

Wilhelm said something in German that seemed to calm the nerves of the passengers, and then another man, as short as he, raced to his side. The two embraced and chattered excitedly.

"I guess this is his brother Jacob?" Sabrina asked. "What are they saying?"

"Wilhelm is trying to explain to him what happened," Granny translated. Then she turned to the rest of the crowd. "I know many of you are confused. You set sail for America expecting to find a relatively unsettled plot of land. Well, you found it. You just didn't show up at the right time."

"What are you talking about, old woman?" Beast growled. "And who are you?"

"My name is Relda Grimm, and this town is Ferryport Landing. It's your home, or at least it will be." Several people rushed to the sides of the ship to gawk out at the little town. "Something unusual has happened. I fear explaining it will be too complicated, but we're hoping we can fix it and send you on your way as soon as possible."

"Did you say your name is Grimm?" Snow White asked as she stepped from the crowd. She was as beautiful as ever. "Are you related to our captains?"

"Yes," Granny replied. "This is my son, Jake, and my granddaughters, Sabrina and Daphne."

The Everafters on the boat roared with approval. "Our savior's family has welcomed us!" a woman called from the back of the crowd. Sabrina peered back and was stunned to find the Queen of Hearts cheering for them.

"Times sure have changed," Sabrina grumbled.

Suddenly, Daphne began to vibrate again. "It's going to happen any minute now," the little girl said.

"We need to get off this boat unless we want to join them in the past," Sabrina added.

"Now?" Puck asked as he flew past the boat. "Do I do it now?"

"Just a moment, Puck," Granny said, then turned back to the passengers. "It appears we really must go."

Uncle Jacob took Briar Rose by the hand. "I'll see you in two hundred years."

The beautiful princess looked confused but flashed him a smile.

Uncle Jake led Granny back to the side of the ship and did his best to help her down. It wasn't as easy as climbing aboard.

"Let my friends help you," Cinderella said. She took three small brown mice from her apron pocket and set them on the ground. Sabrina watched as they morphed into full-grown men, and once the change was complete she recognized them as Malcolm, Alexander, and Bradford—the men who worked on Dr. Cindy's radio show. They helped the family off the ship and down into the rowboat.

"Now?" Puck asked impatiently.

"Now!" Uncle Jake cried once they were safely rowing back toward the shore.

Sabrina watched as Puck pulled the pins on his glop grenades and launched them onto the deck of the ship. They exploded, but not in waves of disgusting filth like last time. These grenades were filled with forgetful dust. Sabrina knew it was necessary to wipe the memories of everyone on the *New Beginning* so that history couldn't be altered, but she still regretted the opportunity they were giving up. They had a chance to change some of the things that made life in Ferryport Landing so hard. Maybe they could have stopped the uprising that led to the barrier's construction. Maybe they could have changed the hatred so many of the Everafters felt for the Grimm family. The possibilities were endless. She watched as the passengers stood on the sides of the boat, glassy eyed; the Beast and his wife, the Frog Prince, Little Bo Peep, and Morgan le Fay. Cinderella and her three assistants waved idly as the ship vanished into the storm.

"I didn't know Dr. Cindy's assistants were the mice from the story," Daphne said, biting her palm in excitement.

"I wonder why they keep it a secret," Granny Relda said.

"I just solved the case!" Sabrina shouted, leaping up from her seat. She was so excited she fell overboard into the cold water. Uncle Jake snatched her by the sleeve and pulled her back into the boat.

"Sabrina! Are you OK?"

"I've solved the mystery!" she said as she wiped water out of her eyes. "I know who stole the magic items."

When they climbed on shore Sabrina explained her theory.

"I don't believe it!" Daphne gasped.

"Dr. Cindy came to our house with her husband, Tom. She must have brought her mice friends, too, and they snuck into the witches' bags," Sabrina said. "The witches unknowingly took them home. That's how they got into everyone's stuff. They went as mice and turned into men to steal the objects!"

"That explains the broken locker at Frau Pfefferkuchenhaus's office," Daphne added. "She must have stuck her bag inside and trapped one of them in there. When he shape-shifted he had to kick the door open from the inside."

"But why? Why would Dr. Cindy need to steal this stuff?"

Uncle Jake asked. "You heard her husband. The radio show is going national. They're going to be rich. They don't need to steal anything."

Mr. Canis was waiting to help everyone back onto shore. His handkerchief was stained through with blood from the slash on his eye.

"Baba Yaga has totally demolished the police station," he informed them. "Nottingham is still alive, for now."

"Good, let her keep him busy," Granny said. "Sabrina has solved the case. We're off to confront the suspect."

The family rushed down the street to the radio station. On top of the building was a huge metal tower with a red light, and above that, another frightening time storm was swirling into existence.

"Uh-oh," Daphne said. She had the magic detector in her hand and she was shaking more intensely than ever before. "People, that's not just a storm. Whatever is going on here is causing the other storms."

They pushed through the doors of WFPR and headed for the stairs, where a sign read STUDIO—3RD FLOOR. But before they reached the first step, they were stopped in their tracks by a huge security guard.

"Can I help you?" he asked, though his tone sounded not at all helpful.

"We need to talk to Dr. Cindy," Granny Relda explained.

"She's on the air right now, so I suggest you give her a call."

"You don't understand," Sabrina said. "She's doing something very dangerous!"

"Listening to callers whine about their miserable lives is hardly risky," the security guard said sarcastically. He reached down and turned a knob on a radio. Dr. Cindy was indeed on the air, trying to help a woman understand that her mother probably didn't love her sister more than her.

"Now, like I said, she's busy," the security guard said roughly. He opened the door and ushered everyone back outside.

"We have to get in there," Daphne said.

"Maybe Mr. Canis could eat the guard," Puck offered.

Canis shrugged as if he were open to the idea.

"I don't think anyone needs to eat anyone," Sabrina said, studying the arsenal of grenades Puck had strapped to his chest. "Got any of those with real glop in them?"

Puck flashed a wicked grin. "Of course."

Uncle Jake propped the door open just a crack. Puck pulled the pin on a grenade and tossed it inside. A second later there was a loud splat and the security guard came running outside, covered in funky-smelling goo. With the guard incapacitated, the family rushed back inside the station and hurried up the steps.

Moments later, they stormed through a door with a sign above it that flashed ON AIR. Dr. Cindy was sitting at a desk speaking into a big microphone hanging from the ceiling. She was wearing a pair of headphones and sipping coffee while she talked to her callers. She looked up in shock when the group barged in, then leaned toward her mic. "And now a word from our sponsors. We'll be right back with more of *The Dr. Cindy Show* in just a moment."

The ON AIR light went dim, and Dr. Cindy took off her headphones. "What's going on? I'm doing a show."

"We know what you're doing," Sabrina said, unconvinced by the woman's dumbfounded expression. "We know all about it."

"Relda, what is this about?" Cindy asked.

"The magic items," Granny said. "Merlin's wand, the Wonder Clock, the water from the Fountain of Youth—"

"We know you stole them," Daphne interrupted.

"Stole them? I've never stolen anything in my life," Cinderella exclaimed. "Relda, I don't know what's going on, but this is incredibly rude, letting your grandchildren come in here and accuse me of being a criminal."

"Cindy, I would agree, but we have evidence. We know your assistants broke into people's homes. They took a handful of low-level magical items, which we believe you have combined to make a new, stronger kind of magic."

"But you don't know what you're doing," Uncle Jake added. "You're causing chaos all over town, and you have stop before you break something no one can fix."

Cindy looked horrified. "You think I sent Malcolm and the others to steal things for me so I could conjure some magic spell? That's outrageous."

"There's an easy way to settle this. We can ask them ourselves," Mr. Canis said.

Puck pulled a grenade off his belt and shook it threateningly in the air. "I'll get them to talk."

"Well, they're not in the studio," Dr. Cindy said, getting up from her chair and storming past the group. "During the broadcast, something went wrong with the transmitter and they're all up on the roof with Tom trying to fix it."

Cindy led them up a flight of steps to the roof. The group was blasted by a heavy wind and blinded by a bright blue light. Sabrina had to shield her eyes just to see two feet in front of her, but soon her sight adjusted. What she saw was shocking. Cindy's husband, Tom Baxter, was standing at the base of the radio tower. Malcolm stood nearby with a tiny glass vial of water. Alexander was blasting the vial with a magic wand. Rays of energy passed through the fluid and onto Tom, who held the clock. Bradford watched the storm above, shouting information to the others about its size and shape. Behind them was the most shocking sight of all: an open black hole, just like the ones Sabrina had seen during the other storms. It was a tear in the fabric of time itself.

"Tom!" Cindy shouted.

Tom's face wrinkled with concern. "Go back downstairs, Cindy. This is very dangerous. It's not safe for you to be up here."

"I'm not going anywhere. What are you doing?" the radio host cried.

"I'm giving us a future," he said with a smile.

"It's happening," Bradford shouted. "The hole is big enough."

Suddenly, there was a brilliant blast from the wand and Tom's body was forced to the very surface of the tear. There, he floated as if he were on his back in a swimming pool. Sabrina, however, felt a tug from the hole, as if it wanted to pull her into its emptiness, too. She noticed that light, loose items were being pulled toward the tear. Stray leaves vanished into the blackness, as well as a couple of scraps of paper.

"You have to stop this," Granny yelled over the wind. "You're meddling in things you have no control over, Tom."

"Don't worry, we've worked everything out," Tom replied. He didn't look the least bit afraid. "It'll all be over soon."

"Mr. Baxter, whatever you're doing here is causing damage to time itself," Sabrina shouted.

"Yes, I know," Tom said. "I hope that wasn't too much of an inconvenience, but it couldn't be helped. Oh, I'm starting to feel it. Alexander, don't let up with that wand."

"What are you trying to make happen, Tom?" Granny cried.

"I built a clock, Relda, a clock that allows me to roll back the years of my life. I'm making myself young again," he said.

Sabrina could see the changes in his appearance. His gray head started to sprout new, brown locks. His posture grew taller and stronger. His shaky hands became still and sure.

"It took us a while to get the proper devices to build my machine," he continued. "Please let everyone know I will return everything and pay for any damages we caused. I didn't want anyone to suffer, but I couldn't think of another way to make this happen."

"Uh-oh," Daphne said as the magic detector started to shake violently. She pointed to the black hole as it doubled in size. Worse, something horrible flew out of the enlarged tear. It was a dragon. It leaped onto the roof, huffed, and then flew into the sky with a head-splitting roar.

"That was the coolest thing I've ever seen," Puck said as he pulled his wooden sword from his waist and released his wings. "I'm going to fight it."

"Forget it! Wait until you get older," Sabrina said as she pulled on his sleeve.

Puck frowned at her. "What are you talking about? I'm an Everafter. I don't get older!" he said, though his voice cracked. He held his throat in shock.

The dragon zipped around the building, leaving a trail of fumes in its wake. Sabrina, Daphne, and Puck had to duck to get out of the way of its sharp claws and long tail.

"Mr. Baxter, you have to stop this. You've already let something out that could kill us all," Uncle Jake shouted. "What's next?"

Tom shook his head. "I just need a little bit longer now," he said as his yellow eyes grew bright and clear. The dark spots on his skin faded, and his stringy arms and legs grew lean and muscular.

Cindy rushed to him and stood close as she could. Her hair and clothes flapped in the tear's greedy pull. "Why are you doing this?"

"Because I love you, Cindy. When I met you I told you I'd love you forever, but my body isn't cooperating with my promise. I'm an old man now, and you are an Everafter, beautiful and unchanged, just like the day I spotted you in the park and forced myself to say hello. My body is withering away. I'm too feeble to even take you on a picnic or dance to our wedding song."

Cindy cried out to him to stop, but her eyes were filled with wonder and possibility. "I love you, Tom, just the way you are!"

"I know you do, Cinderella, and if you didn't I would never have taken this risk. What we have is special—it really could last forever, and I hope you're all right with that. 'Cause when this is over, you're stuck with me for as long as forever takes," Tom said. He placed his feet on the ground, and the energy that had just enveloped him was gone, along with his wrinkles, brittle bones, and thinning hair. Now he was young, strong, and handsome. He didn't look a day over twenty-five. He took Cindy in his arms and kissed her.

The dragon flying overhead let out an angry roar and a series of flaming blasts. The first one hit the transmission tower, and it fell over like a child's toy. Everyone scrambled to get out of the way. The next flare hit a parked car on the street below.

"Uh-oh," Daphne said as the magic detector began to vibrate again.

"What?" Sabrina asked. "Is something else coming through the hole?"

Before Daphne could answer, Tom was violently yanked backward to the edge of the black tear. He squirmed to break free but couldn't.

"Boys, what seems to be the problem?" he called out to his assistants.

Alexander shook the wand, but the power didn't stop. "I can't turn it off," he shouted.

Malcolm slipped the vial into his pocket, but it didn't slow down the chaos. It was almost as if the hole were alive, growing on its own. Even once it had seized Tom, it continued to grow at an alarming rate, and its hunger was ferocious. Leaves and loose papers were no longer enough; it started sucking in everything.

"Can you pull yourself free?" Cinderella asked as she rushed to her husband. He shook his head. She reached up and took his hand, desperately trying to pull him away from the tear's edge, but she wasn't strong enough. She even lost a little gold bracelet as it sailed off her wrist and disappeared into the void.

"I guess it's not finished with me," Tom said, forcing a little laugh. "Honey, you might be married to a teenager pretty soon."

Cindy turned to the family. "Do something!" she cried.

Uncle Jake was already fumbling through his pockets. He pulled out one trinket after another, examined it, and shoved it back into his jacket. "I don't think I've got anything that can stop this."

"Any suggestions?" Sabrina asked her grandmother. Granny's handbag was already swinging toward the hole.

"Perhaps the three of you should go down to the street where it is safe."

"Forget it. I want to see what happens," Puck said.

The fallen transmission tower rolled toward the time hole. Canis grabbed Granny and the girls and leaped over it as it rushed toward them. Luckily, Uncle Jake was not in its path, and Puck flew up into the air to avoid it. A second later, the entire structure was sucked into the tear.

Unfortunately, when Puck rose off the ground to avoid the collision, he found himself trapped in the black hole's gravitational pull. He flapped his wings hard in an effort to escape, but there was nothing for him to grab onto. He drifted closer and closer to the tear with nothing to stop him.

"Uh, we've got a problem," he called.

Sabrina grabbed his foot as he passed, but she, too, was pulled up. "Help!" she yelled. Daphne latched on, and soon the three of them were drifting into the black nothing.

"Children!" Granny cried as she held on for dear life to the side of the building. Both Mr. Canis and Uncle Jake were doing the same. Cindy and her assistants were desperately clinging to a steel pipe. No one could help the children.

Puck drifted into the blackness. His face and upper torso disappeared, then his waist, and finally his knees. All that was left of the boy fairy was his sneakers, which Sabrina clung to with all her strength.

"I'm losing him!" she cried in desperation. "Puck, you have to fight it!"

Without warning, the hole quadrupled in size, threatening to swallow the entire building. From inside came something unexpected—an enormous house sitting on top of two grotesque chicken legs. The house pushed the children back through the hole, but Baba Yaga wasn't inside. Sabrina could see her older self through the window. When the house cleared the event horizon and stepped out onto the roof, the door flew open and the older Sabrina, Daphne, and Puck all leaped out. The older Granny Relda followed in her wheelchair.

"Dear me," Granny exclaimed as she eyed the visitors.

"You've got to close this hole!" the older Daphne shouted as she raced to her younger self. Sabrina studied her sister; there was something different about her. She still wore Uncle Jake's coat, but the scar that once had marred her beautiful face was gone—and even better, the familiar happy light had returned to her eyes.

"Destroy the machine!" the older Granny shouted over the raging storm.

Sabrina and Daphne raced to Malcolm, Alexander, and Bradford.

"Give us the magical items!" Sabrina demanded.

"No! Don't touch it, child!" Tom shouted. "If you destroy it, you'll reverse the process."

"Back off, kid," Malcolm said.

Without a word, Dr. Cindy snatched the Wonder Clock from her husband's hands, lifted it over her head, and brought it down hard on the ground. It splintered into thousands of pieces. The wand suddenly stopped firing, and the wind disappeared. Tom fell from the surface of the hole as it began to shrink.

"Cindy! Why?" he cried, as his body aged rapidly. He tried to stand but stumbled under suddenly frail legs and fell to his knees.

His wife knelt and caressed his face. "Tom, no."

"I did this so we could be together," he said. "You're so young and lively. It's not right for you to be married to someone so old."

Cinderella looked into his eyes. "Then so be it," she whispered, and her body began to age as well. Her long blond hair turned white, wrinkles weaved across her perfect face, and her delicate hands gnarled with arthritis.

"Cindy, no!" Tom cried. "If you age, you can't ever be young again."

"When I married you, I made a promise, too. There's no going back. I wouldn't if I could. You are my prince, and we'll have as much forever as these tired old bodies will allow," Cindy said, her voice rough.

Sabrina's attention turned to the future Puck, who stepped up to his younger self. "Hello, Trickster King," he said as Sabrina's Puck gaped at his older self. "Try to be nicer to Sabrina. She's going to be important to you in the future, and trust me, she'll never forgive you for gluing her head to that basketball."

Puck grinned. "I never glued her head to a basketball."

"You're giving him ideas!" the older Sabrina said reproachfully and kissed her husband.

Mr. Canis and Granny Relda approached the older woman in her wheelchair. Canis bent down and took her hand.

"It's good to see you, old friend," the older Granny said.

"I know what happens. I just don't know when," he said.

"You don't have a lot of time left," the old woman said before breaking into a coughing fit.

"How do I stop it?"

"I'm sorry, but I don't have an answer. We never gave up on you, Tobias."

"Tobias?"

"Oh, sorry, that comes later," the old woman said.

"All right, folks. Looks like the train is leaving the station," the older Puck said as the hole continued to shrink. "If we are going home, we better get going."

"Just a second," the future Daphne said. "I have to call Elvis."

She blasted a whistle with her two fingers, and a second later, the circling dragon descended like a bomb. It crashed to the rooftop and bowed its head to the warrior woman.

"Good boy, Elvis," she said. "Time to go home."

The dragon zipped into the tear and vanished.

"You didn't have a dragon when we last saw you," Sabrina said.

Older Daphne shrugged. "Things change."

The visitors from the future climbed into Baba Yaga's house. Older Sabrina appeared in the window just before the house darted through the tear.

"There are big things ahead, girls. You're going to have to grow up a little," she said.

"We'll try!" Daphne called back.

"Wait! We never found out who causes all the trouble! Who is the Master?"

The older Sabrina shouted something, but the wind was so strong no one could make out the words and a second later, the storm was gone and the hole closed in on itself.

❧

Sabrina's twelfth birthday was embarrassing. Granny Relda made a big deal out of it, forcing her to wear a funny hat that read BIRTHDAY GIRL! in sparkly pink.

Daphne gave Sabrina a princess tiara. Uncle Jake gave her a new pair of sneakers. Mr. Canis, who now wore a bandage on his wounded eye, bought her a little portable radio for her room, and Granny showered her with clothes and a new bicycle. Puck left a box on the kitchen table with her name on it. Inside, she found a basketball and a tube of industrial-strength glue with a note that read:

It's coming when you least expect it.

"Where is the he, anyway?" Sabrina asked.

"In his room pouting," Granny Relda said. "He's not at all happy about his current growth spurt."

"Is he sick?" Daphne asked.

"We're not exactly sure what's causing it," Granny said as she flashed Mr. Canis a knowing smile. "But I have my theories."

"If you think he's a pain now, wait until he starts getting pimples," Uncle Jake said.

Prince Charming also attended the party, indulging in Granny's German chocolate cake. There was music, laughter, and happiness, which had been in short supply as of late. It seemed their recent run-ins with tax bills, Mayor Heart, and Nottingham were just the beginning of their troubles. Everyone feared how the mayor and her sheriff would respond to the Grimms breaking Wilhelm out of prison.

There was a knock at the door. "Who can that be?" Granny asked.

"That's Sabrina's birthday present," Charming said.

Sabrina was surprised. "You got me a birthday present?"

"Go answer the door," he said.

A million ideas raced through her mind. What could the prince have gotten her? She threw open the door and was a little startled to find a strange woman standing on the porch. She had chestnut hair and flawless skin. Her lips were full and her eyes were green. She wore a black suit, pearls, and high-heeled shoes. She oozed sophistication and, aside from Snow White, was easily the most beautiful woman Sabrina had ever seen.

"Are you Sabrina Grimm?" she asked stiffly.

Sabrina nodded.

"My name is Bunny Lancaster," she said. "William sent me."

"OK," Sabrina said, a little dopily. "Are you my present?"

The woman cocked an eyebrow. "I'm not sure what you mean, dear."

Charming appeared at the door. "Bunny, thank you for stopping by. Please come in."

The woman entered and the family gathered around her. "Mrs. Grimm, this is Bunny Lancaster," Charming said.

"I know who she is," the old woman said coolly. Sabrina was surprised by her grandmother's reaction. *Where was the smile? Where was the sweet hello?*

"Are you an Everafter?" Daphne asked, rushing to shake the woman's hand.

Bunny nodded.

"Which one?" Daphne asked, barely able to contain her excitement.

Bunny shifted uncomfortably. "In some circles I have the rather unfortunate title of the Wicked Queen."

"You mean the one who tried to kill Snow White?" Daphne asked, shocked.

"I didn't try to kill her," Bunny said softly.

"Well, Mr. Charming. Thank you for the birthday present, but you shouldn't have. Really, you shouldn't have," Sabrina said.

"Bunny is here to help you," Charming said.

"Help me?"

"Take me to your mirror," the Wicked Queen replied.

"Uh, I'm not sure what you mean," Granny stammered.

"Mrs. Grimm, I am fully aware that you possess a magic mirror," the woman said impatiently. "I also know that Snow voluntarily gave it to your family nearly a hundred years ago. I would like to see it."

Granny glanced at Charming, who nodded as if to say Bunny could be trusted. Relda led the group upstairs and into Mirror's room. When the door closed behind them, the roaring began.

"WHO DARES INVADE MY SANCTUARY!" Mirror's violent face filled the reflection.

"Control yourself," the Wicked Queen said.

"Bunny?" Mirror asked. There was a raw silence between the two. "What a surprise."

The Wicked Queen stepped forward. "Mirror, Mirror can you tell, how to break the sleeping spell?"

"Right down to business, Bunny?" Mirror said. "Very well, a kiss is all it takes."

"That's not what I asked, servant," the woman said sternly. Sabrina bristled at the way the woman was talking to her friend. Mirror shifted, obviously taken aback by the queen's rude tone.

"Bunny, I—"

"Mirror, are you arguing with me?"

"No, I'm—"

"I asked you a question. I expect you to answer it."

"And I answered it," Mirror said.

"No, you did not! Any fool knows a romantic kiss will break a sleeping spell. Do you think I don't know it? I invented this spell. I also know that there is always a back door. What is the back door?"

"I'm not sure what you mean."

The Wicked Queen's right hand began to glow red. Its intensity was blinding, and heat came off it like the fireballs the dragon had breathed the night before.

"Mrs. Grimm, your mirror is defective. Allow me to fix it for you."

"Wait, what are you going to do?" Sabrina demanded.

"The repairs will not harm the contents within, but this guardian is malfunctioning."

"Bunny, don't do anything you'll regret!" Mirror begged.

"What an odd attitude you have," the Wicked Queen said as she placed her red hand on the surface of the mirror. "It's not like I'm going to kill you. You don't exist. You are a creation, with the sole purpose of serving your master's every need. You are not working properly, and I will fix you."

Mirror cried out in pain.

"Leave him alone!" Daphne shouted.

Angry clouds began to gather around Mirror's head. "Leave me be, Mother!"

"Oh, are we back to that, Mirror? I'm not your mother. I am your creator," Bunny said dismissively. "Now, I'm going to ask you again, and this time I want you to give me an answer. Mirror, Mirror, can you tell, how to break the sleeping spell?"

Mirror curled his lip and looked embarrassed. Sabrina wasn't happy, either. Mirror was her friend, and she didn't like strangers

being mean to her friends. She was fully prepared to step between the two of them when Mirror cleared his throat.

"Yes," he said.

"That's more like it!" the Wicked Queen said, then took her hand off the mirror's reflection. It left a bright red handprint that quickly faded away. As it disappeared, so did Mirror's face, and another image replaced it. Sitting in a café on a cobblestone street was a blond woman with short, curly hair. She was sipping coffee and writing in a journal as a waiter tried to get her attention. He smiled at her and said something, but she seemed to be in her own little world.

"There's your answer," the Wicked Queen said.

"Who's that?" Daphne asked.

"Goldilocks," Uncle Jake whispered.

"Goldilocks," Granny repeated.

"Goldilocks indeed," Bunny said, eyeing each member of the Grimm family suspiciously. "It seems as if she has found a way out of our happy little town. Lucky, lucky girl."

Uncle Jake stared at his feet.

"Bunny, I appreciate the help," Charming said as he escorted her out of the room.

"Is she the one Dad was in love with before he met Mom?" Daphne asked.

Granny shuffled her feet.

"Tell her, Mom," Uncle Jake said. "We're not breaking Henry's trust. They both need to know."

Granny ignored him. "Let's say good-bye to our guest."

Everyone left the room except Sabrina. She didn't care about the Wicked Queen or the revelation about her father. She was preoccupied with what had just happened in the room, with someone she trusted.

"Mirror," she said. "I want to talk to you."

Mirror's face appeared in the glass. He looked as if he had just been in a prizefight. "Sabrina—"

"Have you known all along?" Sabrina asked, her voice trembling with anger and hurt.

Mirror shook his head. "No. That's not how—"

"Were you keeping it from us?" She felt like a volcano bubbling over with emotion.

"It's hard to explain, Sabrina. I don't know everything. I'm not omnipotent. If you ask a question I know the answer, but if you don't—

"Are you telling me that I have to be super specific? Mirror, you knew what we wanted to know!"

"I'm not . . . Sabrina, I was the first mirror, the test product," Mirror stammered. "Bunny forgets she didn't give me all the bells and whistles she gave the others. I'm sorry I let you down."

Through her anger, Sabrina could hear the pain in Mirror's voice. It made her feel sorry for him, and her rage faded away.

"It's OK," she said.

Mirror looked as if he might cry. His face faded from the reflection.

"I'm sorry," she said to her own reflection. "I . . . sometimes it's hard to know who to trust in this town. I know you mean well. There is nothing wrong with you. Don't let what she said get to you."

Mirror didn't return.

Sabrina looked down at her mother and father, still slumbering soundly in the bed in the center of the room. "Now all we have to do is find Goldilocks," she said.

She joined everyone at the bottom of the stairs. Bunny was saying her farewells, though Granny and Mr. Canis were keeping their distance. When she opened the door to leave, she found Snow White standing on the porch. The teacher was so stunned, she dropped a glass carousel she was carrying, shattering it into pieces.

"Snow," Bunny said. She waved a hand and the carousel rose into the air, repaired itself, and floated back into the teacher's hands.

"Mother," Snow replied.

"Mother!" the girls shouted in unison.

"Billy?" Ms. White cried when she noticed Prince Charming through the doorway. She looked back and forth at all of them, confused. "Where have you been?"

"I've been busy," Charming said coolly. Sabrina was shocked at his attitude. She knew the prince didn't want to see Ms. White, but she was stunned by how dismissive he sounded.

"I've been . . . I've been worried sick," Ms. White stammered. "I left messages. I've searched everywhere for you."

"You've been wasting your time," Charming said, then looked her in her eyes. "We have both been wasting our time."

"Billy? What's wrong with you?"

"Nothing's wrong with me, Snow. In fact, I've never been better. I finally woke up and remembered how you left me at the altar. You humiliated me in front of my family and friends. What was I thinking when I tried to give you a second chance? Why, I'm wondering if I've been the victim of some black magic."

"Billy! You can't mean that."

"Go home, Snow. You're embarrassing yourself."

Sabrina expected the teacher to turn and run off in tears, but instead she handed her the carousel, then wound up and socked Charming right in the jaw. He stood his ground, but it was obvious that he was in pain.

"You sorry excuse for a man! How could I have been so blind?" Then she turned on Granny Relda. "And you! I thought we were better friends. Hiding Billy, befriending my mother . . . you of all people know what she's done."

"Snow, I—"

Granny never got a chance to explain. Snow stormed down the porch steps and raced off in her car before anyone could stop her.

"Well, it appears I have ruined another party," Bunny muttered. "Happy birthday, young lady."

Moments later, she got into a sleek black sports car and sped away.

Charming walked across the room and snatched his jacket off the couch. He draped it over his own magic mirror, and it vanished into the folds. He thanked the family for letting him stay and headed outside.

"Where are you going?" Granny Relda asked. "You don't have to leave."

"I have things to do, Mrs. Grimm," he said. "And so does your family. You need to make sure Baba Yaga restores her guardians. You need to make her understand that she is vulnerable. The future depends on it."

"That's not going to be so easy," Uncle Jake said. "When I returned her wand she swore my family would be her mortal enemies. I knew we shouldn't have lied to her."

"The witch is moody. Find a way." He turned to the girls. "I have one more present for you, Sabrina, one you can share with your sister. It's advice. No matter the cost, save the ones you love. When you look back, remember these words and you'll know why I did what I had to do."

Sabrina was confused. She wanted to ask him what he meant, but he walked down to the street carrying his jacket.

"Oh, and get the pig's weapon as soon as you can," he called over his shoulder.

A moment later, he was gone.

That night, Sabrina was roused from sleep by incessant knocking on the front door. Later she would wonder why she'd answered it at all. Every time she opened it, she got a nasty surprise. But it was late, and no one else in her family seemed to have heard the visitor. How could she have known that Nottingham and Mayor Heart would be on the other side? How could she have known that both of them would have bloodred handprints painted on their chests.

"So, you're making it official?" Sabrina said. "You've joined the Hand?"

Mayor Heart looked down at the mark. "It is quite an honor to be able to follow the Master. He has great plans for this world."

Granny and Uncle Jake joined Sabrina at the door.

"I've got good news for you, Relda," Heart continued. "We've decided to let you keep your house—for now. I have a feeling we could have raised the tax to a billion dollars and you would still have found a way to pay it. So, congratulations, you are now the last human family in Ferryport Landing. Unfortunately, I have some bad news as well. You see, I tried to be nice and let you leave on your own. But you refused, so now I have to get mean. In the past, you have had Canis to protect you. I suspect that things will get very unpleasant when he isn't around. Nottingham, arrest Canis!"

Nottingham took a pair of handcuffs from his pocket. "Come out, you filthy dog."

"It was my idea to break into the jail and free Wilhelm," Granny said. "Arrest me instead."

"Oh, the jailbreak isn't that important to me," Nottingham said matter-of-factly. "I'm arresting him for murder."

"Murder?" Sabrina cried.

"Yes, he murdered a little girl's grandmother," Nottingham said. "Perhaps you've heard the story?"

"Red Riding Hood?" Uncle Jake said in disbelief. "That was hundreds of years ago."

"Justice is patient," Nottingham said. "Now bring him out. I don't want this to get ugly."

Mr. Canis appeared in the doorway. "I'll go with you, Nottingham," he said calmly, and stepped out of the house. He had no fear or anger in his face. In fact, he seemed at peace.

The sheriff slapped his handcuffs on Canis's huge wrists. "You've got the right to remain silent—" he started.

"You're just giving up?" Sabrina said to Canis. "You could run off. They'd never catch you."

"I joined this family so I could stop running. I'm not about to start again," Canis said. "Besides, it might be safer for everyone if I went away. Tell me, child, was I in prison in the future? If you can change things, I suppose I can as well."

"Whatzgoinon?" Daphne said as she came down the stairs. She was still rubbing the sleep from her eyes.

Sabrina stepped forward. "You won't get away with this. We'll stop you, just like we've stopped the rest of the Scarlet Hand who've crossed us. We've got a whole family. There are only two of you."

"I'm afraid you're mistaken, child," the mayor said as she gestured toward the shadows. "We happen to have some new recruits. Don't be shy," she called. "Come out and say hello."

Sabrina peered into the darkness and saw a mob of Everafters stepping onto their lawn. At the front was the Beast, followed by the Frog Prince and his wife. Miss Muffet stood with her husband, the spider. Tweedledee and Tweedledum were there as well, accompanied by the Cheshire Cat. Glinda the Good Witch stood with them. Behind her was a sea of ogres, witches, trolls, Cyclopes, tree gnomes, leprechauns, and dozens of talking animals. All of them wore red handprints on their chests.

"You look surprised, Grimms. I was hoping you would be," Mayor Heart replied.

"Not surprised—relieved," Sabrina said. "Now I know who the scum are in this town."

"Oh, but there's one more recruit. Allow me to introduce the newest foot solider in the Master's glorious army."

"I'm sure you'll agree he's just a prince of a guy," Nottingham added, and the crowd erupted into laughter.

And from the mob stepped a tall, handsome man with broad shoulders—a man the family knew very well.

"Prince William Charming finally saw the light," Nottingham said.

Charming stepped to the front of the crowd and stood between Mayor Heart and her sheriff. His shirt was marked with a bloodred handprint.

ENJOY THIS
SNEAK PEEK FROM
6

THE SISTERS
GRIMM

~ TALES FROM THE HOOD ~

1

W HAT A CRAZY DREAM," SABRINA MUMBLED when she woke. In it, she had been walking along a stone path until she suddenly realized she was naked. She screamed and rushed to the bushes to hide. How could she have left the house without getting dressed? It was mortifying, but things only got worse. A moment later, Puck appeared. Since she had little alternative, she begged him to bring her a set of clothes. Much to her disbelief, he flew off and swiftly returned with a pair of jeans, a shirt, and sneakers. Then, he walked away so she could dress in private, leaving without so much as a snicker or a sarcastic comment. Relieved, she dressed quickly and continued on her way, only to find people staring and pointing as she passed them. She looked down to find she was completely naked again! She cried out for Puck, hoping he'd fetch her another set of clothing, but the boy fairy just shook his head in disappointment.

"Clothes can't hide who you really are, Sabrina," he said.

Even in her dreams, Puck was a pain.

Now she was awake and, thankfully, dressed in her pajamas. A cool breeze drifted through her bedroom window, causing the model airplanes hanging from the ceiling to sway back and forth. She watched them for a while, imagining her father building them when he was her age. He must have put a lot of effort into the models. They were beautiful.

Sabrina checked her alarm clock: 3:00 a.m. Now was a good time, she decided. There were no emergencies to deal with, no impending chaos, and—best of all—no prying eyes. Her little sister, Daphne, was still asleep, snoring softly into her pillow. She wouldn't wake until morning.

Sabrina slipped out of bed, knelt down, and reached under the bed to a loose floorboard. From beneath it, she retrieved a little black bag. She then tiptoed to the bathroom.

Once there, she closed the door and flipped on the light. Getting the room to herself for more than a few seconds was a special treat. There were a lot of people living in the big old house. In addition to the sisters, there were Uncle Jake, Granny Relda, Puck—and of course Elvis, the family dog, who often used the toilet as a drinking fountain. They all shared one tiny bathroom, and privacy was in short supply.

Sabrina spilled the bag's contents into the sink. It was a small but treasured collection of makeup she quietly bought whenever the family went into town: tubes of lip gloss, eye shadow, mascara, blush, and foundation.

"All right, here goes nothing," she whispered.

First, she smeared on the foundation, but it made her look like a ghost. To balance it out, she put on blush. Then she applied mascara, which was thick and gloppy, and she poked herself in the eye with the eyeliner pencil. After smudging some lipstick on, she took a step back to peer at herself fully the mirror.

Sabrina nearly cried. She looked like the joker from a stack of playing cards. She was hideous. How was she supposed to learn how to use this stuff?

She needed her mother. Veronica would know how to do makeup. She would explain all the things Sabrina was feeling but didn't understand, like why Sabrina's appearance was becoming more and more important to her. It seemed like just yesterday when she couldn't have cared less about how she looked, but now? It felt as if all she could think about was how others might see her. She hated herself for it.

Luckily, no one in her family had noticed her new preoccupation—most importantly Puck. If he discovered she was visiting the bathroom in the middle of the night to primp, he would never stop making fun of her.

Sabrina scrubbed the makeup off her face and was about to go back to bed when she heard something bubbling in the toilet. The lid was down so she couldn't see what was causing the noise, but she had her suspicions. Before Puck had moved into the house with the Grimms, he lived in the woods. Modern conveniences mesmerized him—none more so than the toilet. He loved to flush it over and over and watch the water swirl around and disappear.

For months, he was convinced toilets were some kind of magic, until Uncle Jake explained how plumbing worked. The newfound knowledge only increased Puck's fascination, and it wasn't long before he was conducting "scientific research" to discover what could—and couldn't—be flushed down the tubes. It started out with a little loose change, but the items quickly grew in size: marbles, wristwatches, doorknobs, balls of yarn, even—once—scoops of butter pecan ice cream. Granny finally put an end to the fun when she caught him trying to flush a beaver he'd found in the woods. Ever since, the toilet regularly coughed up Puck's "experiments." Last week Sabrina had found one of her mittens floating in the bowl. Now, apparently, something else was making its way to the surface. She hoped it wasn't the missing TV remote.

But when Sabrina lifted the lid she found something so shocking she would likely fear toilets for the rest of her life. A little man was sitting in the bowl.

"Who goes there?" he demanded in a squeaky voice. He was

less than a foot tall and wore a tiny green suit, a matching bowler hat, and shiny black shoes with brass buckles. His long red beard dipped into the water.

Sabrina shrieked and slammed the toilet lid on the creature's head. He groaned and shouted a few angry curses, but Sabrina didn't stick around to hear them. She ran down the hallway, screaming for her grandmother.

Granny Relda stumbled out of her room wearing an ankle-length nightgown and a sleeping cap. She looked the picture of the sweet, gentle grandmother, except for the sharpened battle-ax she held in her hand.

"*Liebling!*" she cried in a light German accent. "What is all this racket?"

"There's something in the toilet!" Sabrina yelled.

Uncle Jake came out of a room at the end of the hall. He was fully dressed in jeans, leather boots, and his new overcoat, covered with hundreds of little pockets he had sewn himself. He looked exhausted and in dire need of a shave.

"What's all the hubbub?"

"Sabrina saw something in the toilet," Granny Relda explained.

"I swear I flushed," Uncle Jake said as he threw up his hands.

"Not that!" Sabrina shrieked. "It was a person. He spoke to me."

"Mom, you've really got to cut back on all the spicy food you've been feeding the girls," Uncle Jake said. "It's giving them bad dreams."

"It wasn't a dream!" Sabrina insisted. "Come see for yourself."

Daphne entered the hallway, dragging her blanket behind her. "Can't a person get some shut-eye around here?" she grumbled.

"Sabrina had a bad dream," Granny Relda explained.

"It wasn't a dream!" Sabrina repeated. "There's something in the toilet."

"I swear I flushed," Daphne said.

"Ugh! I'll show you," Sabrina said, pulling her family into the bathroom. She pointed at the toilet. "It's in there!"

Granny set her battle-ax on the floor and smiled. "Honestly, Sabrina, I think you're a little old to be scared of the bogeyman."

The old woman lifted the lid. Inside was the little man, rubbing the top of his head and glaring angrily at the crowd.

"What's the big idea?" he growled.

The Grimms all cried out in fright. Startled, Granny slammed the lid down and everyone backed out into the hall.

"Now do you believe me?" Sabrina asked.

"Oh my!" Granny exclaimed. "I'll never doubt you again!"

"What should we do, Mom?" Uncle Jake asked the old woman.

"Elvis!" Granny Relda shouted.

Seconds later, an enormous Great Dane barreled up the stairs, knocking a few pictures off the wall as he bolted to the bathroom. He barked at the toilet fiercely, snarling and snapping at the lid.

"Get him, boy!" Daphne ordered.

"You better surrender!" Uncle Jake shouted at the toilet. "Our dog is very hungry!"

Just then, another door opened down the hall and a shaggyhaired boy in cloud-print pajamas stepped into the hallway. He scratched his armpit and belched. "Is there a war going on out here? Some people are trying to sleep!"

"There's something in the toilet!" Daphne shouted.

"Yeah, I probably forgot to flush," Puck said as he turned back to his room. "Enjoy!"

"Not that! There's a little man in it," Granny Relda said.

"Oh, you mean Seamus," Puck said matter-of-factly. "He's part of your new security detail."

"Security detail?" Sabrina repeated.

"Yeah. Now that Mr. Canis is in jail, you people need bodyguards, and to be honest, I'm too busy to do it all myself. So I hired a team of experts."

"Why is he in the toilet?" Uncle Jake pressed.

"He's guarding it. Duh. The toilet is a vulnerable entrance into this house," Puck explained. "Anything could crawl up the pipes and take a bite of your—"

"We get the idea," Granny Relda interrupted. "What are we supposed to do when we need to use it?"

"Seamus takes regular breaks and has lunch every day at noon," Puck said.

"This is ridiculous," Sabrina said. "We don't need bodyguards, and we definitely don't need you to put some weirdo in the toilet!"

Seamus lifted the lid and crawled out of the toilet with an angry look in his eyes. "Who are you calling a weirdo? I'm a leprechaun. Puck, I didn't sign on for this abuse. I quit!"

"Quit? You can't quit," Puck insisted. "Who will I get to replace you?"

"Go find a toilet elf. What do I care?" the leprechaun shouted as he stomped down the hall, leaving a trail of little wet footprints behind him.

Puck frowned. "Now look what you've done. Do you know how hard it is to find someone to sit in a toilet all day and night?"

"How many more leprechauns are in the house?" Daphne asked, peeking behind the shower curtain.

"That was the only one," Puck said.

"Good!" Sabrina said, relieved.

"But there are a dozen trolls, some goblins, a few elves and brownies, and a chupacabra."

Sabrina gasped. "There are weirdos all over the house?"

"Weirdo is a really ugly term. This is the twenty-first century, you know," Puck replied. "Wait a minute. What's that on your lips?"

Horrified, Sabrina wiped her mouth on her sleeve, leaving a lipstick stain on her shirt. She silently cursed herself for not washing thoroughly enough.

"Puck, we appreciate you looking after us," Granny said. "With Mr. Canis temporarily in the town jail, I guess it can't hurt to have a security detail around the house, but the bathroom might be the one place we don't need an extra set of eyes."

"Suit yourself, but if a dragon crawls up the pipes and toasts your rear end, don't come crying to me," Puck said, stomping off to his room.

Daphne peered into the toilet. "Could a dragon really fit in here?"

Granny Relda assured the little girl that she was safe from dragon attacks and encouraged everyone to go back to bed. "We're going to visit Mr. Canis bright and early tomorrow," she reminded them.

Another wasted trip, Sabrina thought to herself. The family had gone to see their old friend every day since his arrest. Every time, they'd been turned away by the sheriff.

Granny returned to her room, with Elvis trotting behind her.

"Hey, before you two go back to sleep, do you want to see where she is?" Uncle Jake asked.

"Absolutely," Daphne replied.

The girls followed their uncle to a room at the end of the hall. It was sparsely furnished, with only a mirror against the far wall and a queen-size bed in the middle. Lying on the bed were Henry and Veronica Grimm, Sabrina and Daphne's parents, the victims of a spell that kept them sound asleep. Nothing Sabrina and her family had tried could wake them. But recently, the Grimms had found a glimmer of hope—they'd learned a woman from their father's past could break the spell. Unfortunately, this woman wasn't in Ferryport Landing, but the family had found a way to locate her.

The trio turned to the mirror hanging on the wall. This was no ordinary mirror: Instead of their reflection, a huge head with thick features floated in the glass, surrounded by black clouds and streaks of lightning.

"Mirror, we'd like take a look at Goldilocks," Jake said.

"Jake, you know how this works. Poetry activates the magic," Mirror replied.

Daphne stepped forward. "Mirror, Mirror, my greatest wish is to know where Goldilocks is."

Mirror frowned.

"What?" Daphne said. "It rhymes!"

"Hardly! *Is* and *wish* do not rhyme."

"It's close enough!"

"Where is the rhythm? And the meter—atrocious!"

"Listen, if you want real poetry, read some Maya Angelou," Uncle Jake said. "Just show us Goldilocks."

Mirror frowned but did as he was told. Gazing into the silvery surface, Sabrina saw a beautiful, curly-haired woman appear. She had a round face and green eyes. Her button nose was painted with a splash of freckles, and her blond hair looked like sunshine. She wore a billowy white dress and was perched atop a camel. There were other people with her, each on their own camel. Everyone was snapping pictures of an ancient pyramid rising out of a rocky desert.

"Goldilocks," Sabrina whispered.

"Wherever she is, it looks hot," Daphne said, peering into the mirror.

"I think it's Egypt. The place is overrun with pyramids," Uncle Jake said.

"Last week she was in the Serengeti, the week before—South Africa." Daphne said.

Uncle Jake shrugged. "She's only ever in one place for a few days and then she jets off somewhere completely different."

"How are we going to get a message to her?" Sabrina growled. "She has to come back here. She has to help us wake up Mom and Dad!"

Daphne and Uncle Jake seemed taken aback by Sabrina's sudden temper, but she had a right to be angry. Their mission to break the sleeping spell had once felt hopeless. Now they had a solution, and it was almost harder than before. Watching Goldilocks dart around the world on her silly vacations and not being able to speak to her was maddening.

"Be patient, 'Brina," Uncle Jake said soothingly. "We'll track her down."

Mirror's fierce face appeared in the silver surface.

"Is there anything else I can help you with, folks?" Mirror asked.

"Not unless you can drag Goldilocks away from Egypt and bring her here," Jake said.

"I'm afraid that's not one of my abilities. Speaking of dragging, though—girls, could you drag your uncle out of here? He's been lurking in front of me for two weeks. He needs something to eat and, if you ask me, a long-overdue bath."

"Mirror!" Uncle Jake cried.

Daphne sniffed the air. "You are a little rank."

Uncle Jake sighed and threw his hands up in surrender. "Fine! I get it! You two should run off to bed. You heard your grandmother: You've got another big day tomorrow of sitting outside the jail, hoping to see Mr. Canis."

"You're not coming with us?" Daphne asked her uncle.

"Not this time, peanut. I've got plans."

"Briar Rose plans?" Sabrina asked.

"Holding hands and smooching plans?" Daphne asked.

"If I play my cards right." Uncle Jake winked. "Girls, I have to confess. I think the princess is the one."

Daphne's face cracked into a wide grin. "I call dibs on being the flower girl at the wedding."

"Let's not get too far ahead of ourselves," Uncle Jake said, but he was grinning just as widely.

ABOUT THE AUTHOR

Michael Buckley is the *New York Times*–bestselling author of the Sisters Grimm and NERDS series, *Kel Gilligan's Daredevil Stunt Show*, and the Undertow Trilogy. He has also written and developed television shows for many networks. Michael lives in Brooklyn, New York, with his wife, Alison; their son, Finn; and their dog, Friday.